THE SWITCH

D1304907

ANTHONY HOROWITZ

PUFFIN BOOKS
An Imprint of Penguin Group (USA) Inc.

PUFFIN BOOKS
Published by the Penguin Group
Penguin Young Readers Group, 345 Hudson Street, New York, New York 10014, U.S.A.
Penguin Group (Canada), 90 Eglinton Avenue East, Suite 700, Toronto, Ontario, Canada M4P 2Y3
(a division of Pearson Penguin Canada Inc.)
Penguin Books Ltd, 80 Strand, London WC2R 0RL, England
Penguin Ireland, 25 St Stephen's Green, Dublin 2, Ireland (a division of Penguin Books Ltd)
Penguin Group (Australia), 250 Camberwell Road, Camberwell, Victoria 3124, Australia
(a division of Pearson Australia Group Pty Ltd)
Penguin Books India Pvt Ltd, 11 Community Centre, Panchsheel Park, New Delhi - 110 017, India
Penguin Group (NZ), 67 Apollo Drive, Rosedale, North Shore 0632, New Zealand
(a division of Pearson New Zealand Ltd.)
Penguin Books (South Africa) (Pty) Ltd, 24 Sturdee Avenue,
Rosebank, Johannesburg 2196, South Africa

Registered Offices: Penguin Books Ltd, 80 Strand, London WC2R 0RL, England

First published in Great Britain by Walker Books Ltd.
First published in the United States of America by Philomel Books,
a division of Penguin Young Readers Group, 2009
Published by Puffin Books, a division of Penguin Young Readers Group, 2010

1 3 5 7 9 10 8 6 4 2

THE LIBRARY OF CONGRESS HAS CATALOGED THE PHILOMEL BOOKS EDITION AS FOLLOWS:
Horowitz, Anthony, 1955—
The switch / Anthony Horowitz. p. cm.
Summary: When wealthy, spoiled, thirteen-year-old Tad Spencer wishes he were someone else, he
awakens as Bob Snarby, the uncouth, impoverished son of carnival workers, and as he is drawn into a
life of crime he begins to discover truths about himself and his family.
ISBN 978-0-399-25062-0 (HC)
[1. Supernatural—Fiction. 2. Identity—Fiction. 3. Criminals—Fiction. 4. Carnivals—Fiction.
5. Wealth—Fiction. 6. Cosmetics industry—Fiction. 7. England—Fiction.] I. Title.
PZ7.H7875Swi 2009 [Fic]—dc22 2008032380

Puffin Books ISBN 978-0-14-241547-4

Printed in the United States of America

Wishing on a star

Tad was in a bad mood when he went to bed. Dressed in his brand-new silk pajamas, he flicked off the light and slid himself between the crisply laundered Irish linen sheets. The trouble was that he was a boy who had everything. And he was used to having everything. He expected it.

"It's not fair," he muttered. His head sank back into his goose-feather pillow. Moonlight slid across the wall and onto his pale, scowling face. "Why can't I go to the theme park? Why can't I do what I want to do?"

Suddenly Snatchmore Hall seemed like a prison to him. His parents, his great wealth, his school and his surroundings were just the shackles that bound him, and he wanted none of it.

"I wish I was somebody else," he muttered to himself.

And 127 million light-years away, a star that had been burning white suddenly glowed green, just for a few seconds, before burning white again.

But Thomas Arnold David Spencer hadn't seen it. He was already asleep.

ALSO BY ANTHONY HOROWITZ

THE ALEX RIDER NOVELS

Stormbreaker

Point Blank

Skeleton Key

Eagle Strike

Scorpia

Ark Angel

Snakehead

Crocodile Tears

THE DIAMOND BROTHERS MYSTERIES

Public Enemy Number Two

The Falcon's Malteser

Three of Diamonds

South by Southeast

The Greek Who Stole Christmas

The Complete Horowitz Horror

The Devil and His Boy

Granny

Groosham Grange

Return to Groosham Grange: The Unholy Grail

THE SWITCH

For Jill, with love

CONTENTS

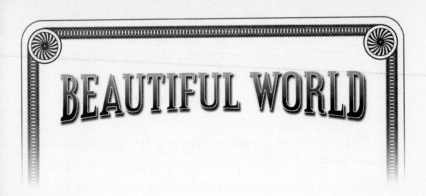

BEAUTIFUL WORLD

The white Rolls-Royce made no sound as it sped along the twisting country road. It was the middle of summer and the grass was high, speckled with wild poppies and daisies. Sunlight danced in the air. But the single passenger in the back of the car saw none of it. His head was buried in a book: *My 100 Favorite Equations.* As he flicked a page, he popped another cherry marzipan chocolate into his mouth, the fourteenth he had eaten since Ipswich. The automatic window slid open and yet another chocolate wrapper was whipped away by the wind. It twisted briefly in the air, then fell. By the time it hit the ground, the Rolls was already out of sight. And Thomas Arnold David Spencer was a little nearer home.

Thomas Arnold David—Tad for short—was thirteen years old, dressed in gray trousers that were a little too tight for him, a striped tie and blue blazer. He had short black hair, rather too neatly combed, and deep brown eyes. He was returning home from Beton Academy on this, the first day of summer vacation. It was typical of Tad that he should have started his homework already. Tad loved homework. He was only sorry he hadn't been given more.

The Rolls-Royce paused in front of a set of wrought-iron gates. There was a click and the gates began to open automatically. At the same time a video camera set on a high brick wall swiveled around to watch the new arrival with a blank, hostile eye. Beyond the gates, a long drive stretched out for almost half a mile between lawns that had been rolled perfectly flat. Two swans circled on a glistening pond, watching the Rolls as it continued forward. It passed a rose garden, a vegetable garden, a croquet lawn, a tennis court and a heated swimming pool. At last it stopped in front of the fantastic pile that was Snatchmore Hall, home of the Spencer family. Tad had arrived.

The chauffeur, a large, ugly man with hooded eyes, crumpled cheeks and a small snub nose, got out of the car and held the door open for Tad. "Glad to be home, Master Spencer?"

"Yes, thank you, Spurling." Tad's voice was flat, almost emotionless. "Rather."

"I'll take your suitcases to your room, Master Spencer."

"Thank you, Spurling. Just leave them on the bed."

Tad went over to the swimming pool, where a bored-looking woman was lying on a sun lounger, gazing at herself intently in a small mirror. This was his mother, Lady Geranium Spencer.

"Good afternoon, Mother," Tad said. He knew not to kiss her. It would have ruined her makeup.

"Oh, hello, dear." His mother sighed. "Is it vacation already?"

"Yes."

"Oh. I thought it was next week. What do you think of the nose?"

"It's jolly good, Mother. They've moved it a little, haven't they?"

"Yes. Just a teensy-weensy bit to the left." Lady Spencer had visited no fewer than six plastic surgeons that spring and each one of them had operated on her nose, trying to give her the exact look she required. Now she was sure she had at last gotten it right. The only trouble was that she wasn't allowed to sneeze until Christmas. "How was school, darling?" she asked, putting the mirror away.

"It was fine, thank you, Mother. I had the highest grade in the class in French, English, chemistry, math and Latin. Second in Ancient Greek and geography. Third in—"

"Ah! Here's Mitzy with the tea!" his mother interrupted, stifling a yawn. "Just what I fancied. A teensy-weensy tea."

The front door of the house had opened and a trolley, piled high with cakes and sandwiches, had appeared, seemingly moving by itself. As it drew closer, however, a tiny woman could be seen behind it, wearing a black dress with a white apron. This was Mitzy, the family's servant for the past forty years.

"Hello, Master Tad!" she gurgled breathlessly as she

heaved the trolley to a halt. It was so heavy it had left deep tire tracks across the lawn.

"Hello, Mitzy." Tad smiled at her. "How are you?"

"I can't complain, Master Tad."

"And Bitzy?" This was Mitzy's husband. His real name was Ernest but he had been given his nickname after he'd been blown to pieces by a faulty gas main.

"He's still in the hospital." Mitzy sighed. "I'm seeing him on Sunday."

"Well, do give him my regards," Tad said cheerfully, helping himself to a smoked-salmon roll.

Mitzy limped back to the house while Tad ate. Lady Spencer cast a critical eye at her son. "Have you put on weight?" she asked.

"Just a little, Mumsy. I'm afraid you're going to have to buy me a completely new uniform for next term. This one's much too tight."

"What a bore! That's the third this year."

"I know. The elastic on my underpants snapped during the headmaster's speech. It was rather embarrassing . . ."

Just then there was a loud bark and a dog bounded across the lawn toward Tad and his mother. It was a dalmatian—you could easily tell that from its black-and-white coat—but it was like no dalmatian you had ever seen.

For a start, it was huge. Its teeth were incredibly sharp and its mouth, instead of grinning in the friendly way ordinary dalmatians do, was twisted in an ugly frown. The reason for all this was that the Spencers had taken the unfortunate dog

4

to a vet who had turned it into a killing machine, filing both its teeth and its claws until they were needle-sharp. The last burglar who had tried to break in had needed 107 stitches when Vicious had finished with him. In the end the police surgeon had run out of thread and had been forced to use glue.

But Vicious recognized Tad. Panting and whimpering, the dog sat down and raised a paw, its eyes fixed on the tea trolley.

"Hello, Vicious. How are you?" Tad reached out with an éclair. The dog leaped up and half of Tad's arm disappeared down its throat as Vicious sucked the éclair free.

"You spoil that dog," his mother remarked.

After tea, Tad went up to his room, taking the elevator to the third floor. Spurling had carried his suitcases up and Mrs. O'Blimey, the Irish housekeeper, had already unpacked them. Tad sat down on his four-poster bed and looked around contentedly. Everything was where it should be. There were his two computers and fourteen shelves of computer games. There was his portable television plugged into his own video recorder and satellite system. His favorite books (Dickens and Shakespeare), bound in leather and gold, stretched out in a long line over his butterfly collection, his stereo and interactive CD system and his tank of rare tropical fish. Then there were nine closets containing his clothes and next to them a door leading into his private bathroom, sauna and Jacuzzi.

Tad stretched out his arms and smiled. He had the whole summer vacation to look forward to. As well as the country house in Suffolk, there was the villa in the south of France, the penthouse in New York and the mews house in Knightsbridge, just around the corner from Harrods. He unbuttoned his jacket and took it off, letting it fall to the floor. Mrs. O'Blimey could pick it up later. It was time for dinner. And soon his father would be home.

In fact Sir Hubert Spencer didn't get in until after nine o'clock. He was a large, imposing man with wavy silver hair and purple blotches on his cheeks, nose and hands. He was dressed, as always, in a plain black suit cut from the very finest material. As he strode into the room and sat down he pulled out an antique pocket watch and glanced at the face.

"Good evening, Tad," he said. "Good to see you. Now. I can give you nine and a half minutes . . ."

"Gosh! Thank you, Father."

Tad was delighted. He knew that his father was a busy man. In fact, business ruled his life.

Ten years ago, Sir Hubert Spencer had set up a chain of shops that now stretched across England, Europe and America. The shops were called simply Beautiful World and sold soaps, shampoos, body lotions, sun creams, vitamins, minerals, herbs and spices . . . everything to make you feel beautiful inside and out. What made these shops special, however, was that the ingredients for many of the products came from the Third World—yak's milk from the mountain villages of Tibet, for example, or crushed orchids from the tropical rain forests of Sumatra. And all the shops carried a sign in large letters in the window:

Sir Hubert had realized that people not only wanted to look good, they wanted to feel good too. And the better they felt, the more they would spend and the richer he would become.

Sir Hubert never stopped. He was always developing new products, finding new ingredients, dreaming up new advertising ideas, selling more products. It was said that while he was being knighted by the queen, two years before, he had managed to sell her ten gallons of face cream and a lifetime's supply of Japanese seaweed shampoo. He had appeared on the front page of all the newspapers after that. Because, despite his great wealth, Sir Hubert was very popular. "Good old Sir Hubert!" people would shout out if they saw him in the street. "He may be stinking rich, but he's all right."

The reason for this popularity—and also for his knighthood—was his charity work. At about the same time that he had set up Beautiful World, he had started a charity called ACID. This stood for the Association for Children in Distress and was based in London. ACID aimed to help all the young people who had run away or been abandoned in the city, giving them shelter and providing them with food or clothes. Tad himself had donated two pairs of socks and a Mars bar to the charity. He was very proud of his father and dreamed of the day when, maybe, he would be knighted too.

"Sorry I'm late," Sir Hubert announced now as he sat himself down in his favorite armchair beside the fire with Vicious curled up at his feet. "We've got problems with our new Peruvian cocoa-leaf bubble bath. Not enough bubbles. We may have to do more tests . . ." He turned to Spurling, who was standing beside him. "Have you poured me a brandy, Spurling?"

"Yes, Sir Hubert."

"Have you warmed it for me?"

"Yes, Sir Hubert."

"Well, you can drink it for me too. I haven't got time."

"Certainly, Sir Hubert." Taking the glass, the chauffeur bowed and left the room.

Sir Hubert turned to Tad, who was playing Scrabble with Lady Spencer. Tad was a little annoyed. He had a seven-letter word but unfortunately it was in Ancient Greek. "So, Tad," he exclaimed. "How was school?"

"Jolly good, Father. I got the highest grade in French, English, chemistry, math and Latin. Second in—"

"That's the spirit!" Sir Hubert interrupted. "Now. What have you got planned for the summer?"

"Well, I was thinking about going on safari in Africa, Father."

"Didn't you do that last summer?"

"Yes. But it was rather fun. One of the guides got eaten by a tiger. I got some great photos."

8

"I thought you wanted to go to the Red Sea."

"We could do that afterward, Father."

"Oh—all right." Sir Hubert turned to his wife. "You'd better take the boy to Harrods and get him some tropical clothes," he said. "Oh—and some scuba-diving lessons."

"And there is one other thing, Father."

"What's that, Tad?" There was a jangling sound from Sir Hubert's top pocket and he pulled out one of his cell phones. "Could you hold the line, please," he said. "I'll be with you in . . . ninety-three seconds."

Tad took a deep breath. "Rupert said he'd come up this week. You know—he's my best friend. And we thought we might go to Maple Towers together."

"Maple Towers?"

"It's that new theme park that's just opened. It's got an amazing new ride—the Monster. Apparently it's almost impossible to go on it without throwing up—"

"A theme park?" Sir Hubert considered, then shook his head. "No. I don't think so."

"What?" Tad stared at his father. Perhaps unsurprisingly, *no* was his least favorite word.

"No, Tad. These theme parks seem very vulgar to me. Why don't you go horse-racing at Ascot?"

"I'll do that too, Father."

"What about flying lessons? You've hardly touched that two-seater plane I bought you—"

"I will, Father, but—"

"No. I don't want you going on those rides. They're

9

dangerous and they're noisy. And all those people! You're a sensitive boy, Tad. I'm sure they're not good for you."

"But, Father! Mother . . . !"

"I have to agree with your father," Lady Spencer said. She looked at her Scrabble letters, which she had been studying for the past ten minutes. "Is *zimpy* a word?" she asked.

Tad was in a bad mood when he went to bed. Dressed in his brand-new silk pajamas, he flicked off the light and slid himself between the crisply laundered Irish linen sheets. The trouble was that he was a boy who had everything. And he was used to having everything. He expected it.

"It's not fair," he muttered. His head sank back into his goose-feather pillow. Moonlight slid across the wall and onto his pale, scowling face. "Why can't I go to the theme park? Why can't I do what I want to do?"

Suddenly Snatchmore Hall seemed like a prison to him. His parents, his great wealth, his school and his surroundings were just the shackles that bound him, and he wanted none of it.

"I wish I was somebody else," he muttered to himself.

And 127 million light-years away, a star that had been burning white suddenly glowed green, just for a few seconds, before burning white again.

But Thomas Arnold David Spencer hadn't seen it. He was already asleep.

THE CARAVAN

Tad knew something was wrong before he'd even opened his eyes.

First there was the sound, a metallic pattering that seemed to be all around him: frozen peas falling on a tin plate. That was what had woken him up. At the same time he became aware of the smell. It was a horrible smell—damp and dirty—and the worst thing was that it seemed to be coming from him. He moved slightly and that was when he knew that something had happened to the bed too. The sheets were wrinkled and rubbed against his skin like old newspaper. And the pillow . . . ?

Tad opened his eyes. His face was half buried in a pillow so utterly disgusting that he was almost sick. It was completely shapeless, stuffed with what felt like old rags. It had no pillowcase, and though it might once have been white, it was now stained with dried-up puddles of sweat and saliva, various shades of yellow and brown. Tad pushed it off his face, gasping for air.

He looked up, staring through the gray light. But what he saw made no sense. His brain couldn't take it in. He lay there, unable to move.

Instead of the chandelier that should be hanging over his bed, there was a neon tube with a tangle of naked wires twisting out of a broken plastic fitting. The sound of the frozen peas, he now realized, was rain hitting the walls and the ceiling. He was lying in a small bed in the corner of a small room in . . . it had to be a caravan. He could tell from the shape of the walls. There was a window with no curtains, but he couldn't see out because the glass was the frosted sort that you sometimes get in bathrooms or toilets. The room was very cold. Tad drew his legs up and the bed creaked and groaned.

The room was only a little larger than the bed itself, divided from the rest of the caravan by a plastic-covered wall with a door. Somebody had left some clothes crumpled in a heap on the floor. A pair of torn and soiled jeans poked out from a tangle of T-shirts, socks and underwear. There were also some comics, a battered ghetto blaster and a few toys, broken, missing their batteries.

How had he gotten here? Tad tried to think, tried to remember. He had gone to bed like he always did. Nothing had happened. So how . . . ? There could only be one answer. He had been kidnapped. That had to be it. Someone had broken into Snatchmore Hall, getting past the wall, the moat, the security system and the dog, had drugged him while he was asleep and kidnapped him. He had read about this sort of thing happening. His father would have to pay some money—a ransom—but that was no problem because Sir Hubert had lots of money. And then he would be allowed to go home.

The more Tad thought about it, the more relieved he became. In fact, it was almost exciting. He'd be on the television and in all the newspapers: **MILLIONAIRE'S SON IN RANSOM DEMAND, BOY HERO RETURNS HOME SAFE**. That would certainly be something to tell them when he got back to school! And when the kidnappers were finally caught (as of course they would be), he would have to go to court. He would be the star witness!

Tad glanced at his watch, wondering what time it was. The watch was gone. That didn't surprise him. It was a Rolex, solid gold, with a built-in calendar, calculator and color TV. His mother had given it to him a year ago to thank him for tidying up his room when Mrs. O'Blimey was out sick. The wretched kidnappers must have taken it. (They also seemed to have taken his silk pajamas—he was wearing only pants and a black T-shirt that was several sizes too big.) Tad lowered his hand—then raised it again. Was he going crazy . . . or was his wrist thinner than it had been? With an uneasy feeling in his stomach, he closed his third finger and his thumb in a circle around where his watch had once been. They met.

Tad began to tremble. How long had he been in the caravan? Could it have been weeks—even months? How had he managed to lose so much weight?

Cautiously, he swung himself out of the bed. His bare feet came to rest on a carpet so old and dirty that it was impossible to tell what color it had once been. The smell of stale cigarette smoke hung in the air. Tiptoeing, one step at a time, he crossed the room, making for the door.

His hand—the hand was thinner too, just like his wrist—closed around the doorknob and slowly he turned it. The door was unlocked. Tad opened it and stepped into a second room, larger than the first and shrouded in darkness.

This room was dominated by a large fold-down bed—he could just make out its shape as his eyes got used to the gloom—and now he realized there were two people inside it, buried beneath a blanket that rose and fell as they breathed. One of the figures was snoring loudly. Tad was sure it was a woman. Her breath was rattling at the back of her throat like a cat flap in the wind. The man next to her muttered something in his sleep and turned over, dragging the cover with him. The woman, still asleep, groaned and pulled it back again. Tad stepped forward, his foot just missing an empty whiskey bottle on the floor. The wall on the other side of the room was nothing more than a ragged curtain, hanging on a rail. He had to get to it before the two people—his kidnappers—woke up.

He forced himself to take it slowly, making no sound. He was helped at least by the rain. It was coming down more heavily now, striking the metal roof of the caravan and echoing throughout, the noise masking the sound of his own footsteps as he edged around the bed. At last he reached the curtain. He padded at the material until he found a gap and, with a surge of relief, passed through.

He found himself now in the third and last section of the caravan. It was without a doubt the most disgusting part of all.

It was a kitchen, shower and toilet combined, with all the different articles of those rooms jumbled up together. There were dirty pots and pans stacked up in the shower and used, soggy towels next to the sink. A roll of toilet paper had unspooled itself over the oven and there were two grimy bars of soap, a razor and a toothbrush on top of the stove. Unwashed plates, thick with food from supper the night before, lay waiting on a shelf over the toilet while the oven door hung open to reveal two washcloths, a sponge shaped like a duck and a hairbrush that was matted with curling black hair. All the walls and the ceiling were coated with grease and there were pools of water and more hair on the floor. Tad was amazed that anyone could live like this. But it wasn't his problem. He just wanted to get out.

And there was the front door! He was amazed that it was as easy as this. All he had to do was get out the door and run. He would make it to the nearest telephone and call the police. Tad took one step forward. And that was when he saw the other boy.

The boy was thin and pale and about a year younger than Tad. He had long fair hair that hung in greasy strands over a rather sickly-looking face dotted with acne. His right ear was pierced twice with a silver ring and a stud shaped like a crescent moon. The boy could have been handsome. He had bright blue eyes, full lips and a long, slender neck. But he looked hungry and dirty and there was something about his expression that was pinched and mean. Right now he was standing outside the caravan, staring at Tad through a small window.

Tad opened his mouth to cry out. The boy did the same.

And that was when Tad knew, with a sense of terror, that he wasn't looking at a window. He was looking at a *mirror*. And it wasn't a boy standing outside the caravan. It was his reflection!

It was him!

Tad stared at himself in the mirror, watched his mouth open to scream. And he did scream—a scream that wasn't even his voice. His hands grabbed hold of his T-shirt and pulled it away from him as if he could somehow separate himself from the body that was beneath it.

His body.

Him.

Impossible!

"Whass all this racket, then? Whass going on?"

Tad spun around and saw that the curtain had been pulled back. Before him stood a man, wearing a pair of stained pajama bottoms but no top. His naked stomach was dangling over the waistband, a nasty rash showing around the belly button. The man's face was pale and bony and covered with a gingery stubble that matched what was left of his hair. His eyes were half closed. One of them had a sty bulging red and swollen under the lid. There was a cigarette dangling from his lips and Tad realized with a shiver of disgust that he must have slept with it there all night.

"Who are you?" Tad gasped.

"Whaddya mean who am I? What the devil are you talking about?"

"Please. I want to go home . . ."

The man stared at Tad as if he was trying to work him out. Then suddenly he seemed to understand. A slow, nasty smile spread across his face, making the cigarette twitch. "You been at the glue again," he muttered.

"What?" Tad's legs were giving way beneath him. He had to lean against the wall.

Then a voice called out from the other side of the curtain. "Eric? What is it?" It was a woman's voice, loud and shrill.

"It's Bob. 'E's been sniffing the glue again. I reckon 'e's 'ad an 'ole tube full. And now 'e doesn't know 'oo 'e is or where 'e is."

"Well, slap some sense into 'im and throw 'im in the shower," the voice cried out. "I want my breakfast."

"I'm not Bob," Tad whimpered. "There's been a mistake."

But before he could go on, the man had grabbed hold of him, one hand closing around his throat. "There was a mistake all right!" the man snarled. "And what was it? Model airplane glue? Well, you'd better get your head in order, you little worm. 'Cause it's your turn to wash up and make breakfast!" And with that, the man threw Tad roughly into the corner, spat out the cigarette and went back into the bedroom, drawing the curtain behind him.

Tad stayed where he was for a long time. His heart was racing so fast that he could hardly breathe. He looked at his hands again, his stomach, his legs. With trembling fingers, he touched his cheeks, his eyebrows, his hair, tugged at the two pins in his right ear. He let his hands fall and gazed at his palms. He knew, even without understanding why, that he had never seen those hands before. They weren't his hands.

Somehow, something horrible had happened. He had gone to sleep as Tad. *But he had woken up as Bob.*

A few minutes later the curtain was drawn back and a woman came out.

She was one of the ugliest women Tad had ever seen. For a start, she was so fat that the caravan rocked when she moved. Her legs, swathed in black stockings, were thin at the ankles but thicker than tree trunks by the time they disappeared into her massive, exploding bottom. She had arms like hams in a butcher shop, and as for her face, it was so fat that it seemed to have swallowed itself. Her squat nose, narrow eyes and bright red lips had sunk into flabby folds of flesh. Her hair was black and tightly permed. She wore heavy plastic earrings, a wooden necklace and a variety of metal bangles, brooches and rings.

She took one look at Tad and shook her head. The earrings rattled. "Gawd's truth!" she muttered to herself. Then suddenly she lashed out with her foot. Tad cried aloud as her shoe caught him on the hip. "All right, you," the woman exclaimed. "If you're not going to 'elp, you can clear out. Go out and be sick or something. That'll straighten you out."

"Please . . ." Tad began, getting to his feet.

"I told you that glue was no good for you. But would you

listen? No! You get yourself dressed . . ." The woman snatched a handful of clothes from the top of the fridge and threw them at Tad. "Now get out, Bob. I don't wanna see you again until you got your act together."

"No. You don't understand . . ."

But the woman had clenched her fist and Tad realized she didn't want to know. Clutching the clothes, he scrabbled for the door, found the handle and turned it. Behind the woman, the man had appeared, now wearing a knit shirt and jeans and smoking a fresh cigarette. He saw what was happening and laughed. "You show 'im, Doll!" he called out.

"Shut up!" his wife replied.

Tad fell through the door and into his new world.

THE CARNIVAL

Tad was standing in the middle of a carnival that
had been set up on a patch of lumpy ground near a main road.
There were about a dozen rides and the usual shooting galler-
ies and sideshows. But everything was so old and broken
down, with flaking paint and broken lightbulbs, that it didn't
look like fun at all. The carnival was completely encircled by
a cluster of caravans and trucks, some with electric generators.
Thick cables snaked across the ground, joining everything to
everything in a complicated tangle. There was nobody in
sight.

Although the rain had eased off, it was still drizzling and
this, along with the gray light of early morning, only made the
scene more wretched. Tad felt the water dripping down his
arms and legs and remembered that he was almost naked.
Hastily he sorted through the clothes the woman had thrown

him—a pair of jeans, faded and torn at the knees, a sweater, socks and sneakers. Holding them up in front of him, Tad knew at once that they were much too small. There was no way they could possibly fit him. But when he did finally pull them on, they did!

Tad looked back at the caravan. It was one of the largest in the carnival. Once it had been white, but rust had eaten away most of the paintwork and dirt covered what little was left. The door was still firmly shut, but there was a buzzer next to it and below that a slip of paper under a plastic cover. It read:

ERIC AND DOLL SNARBY

Doll. That was what the man had called the woman. Next to the nameplate somebody had added three letters, gouging them into the side of the caravan.

BOB

Tad ran his finger along it and swallowed hard. Bob Snarby. Was that who he was?

"I am not Bob Snarby! I'm Tad Spencer!"

But even as he spoke the words, he knew that they weren't true. Like it or not, something had happened, and for the time being anyway, he was this other boy. He was also very hungry. The smell of bacon was seeping out under the caravan door.

He could almost hear it sizzling in the pan. He had no money and no idea where he was. But breakfast was cooking on the other side of the door. What choice did he really have?

Tad opened the door and went back in.

Doll Snarby was sitting, wedged behind the table, with a mountain of eggs, bacon, sausages and toast in front of her. As Tad came into the room she pronged a whole fried egg on her fork and slipped it into her mouth, a trickle of grease dribbling down her chin. Eric Snarby was at the stove, a new cigarette between his lips. He had a bad cough. In fact he was spluttering as much as the bacon in the pan.

"So you come back in, 'ave you," Eric coughed. "Just like you to shove off when it's your turn to do the cooking."

"Don't be cruel to the boy," Doll Snarby shouted. She reached out and jabbed Tad hard in the ribs. "That's *my* job!"

"I suppose you want some bacon?" Eric asked.

"Yes, please," Tad said.

"Oh! *Please!*" Eric sang the word in a falsetto voice. "'Aven't we got airs and graces today." He coughed again, spraying the bacon with spittle. "'E'll be saying 'thank you' next an' all!"

"Leave the little maggot alone," Doll said. She slid an empty plate in front of Tad.

Tad looked down. The plate was coated in grease and dried gravy from the night before. "This is dirty," he said.

Doll scowled. "Well, there's no point washing it, is there!" she said reasonably. "You're only going to put more food on it."

Eric Snarby slid two lumps of bacon, a fried egg and a piece of fried bread onto Tad's plate. Doll picked up two pieces of toast, emptied half a jar of marmalade between them and pressed them into a sandwich. Eric had made himself a cup of tea and sat next to his wife.

She sniffed at him. "You smell!" she exclaimed.

"So what?" he replied, the eye with the sty twitching indignantly.

"Why don't you 'ave a barf?" his wife complained.

"Because we don't 'ave a barf," Eric Snarby replied. "And I'm not going in the shower. Not till you take out your panties!"

Tad tried not to listen to any of this but instead concentrated on his breakfast. He had never seen food like it. Back home at Snatchmore Hall, breakfast would have been freshly squeezed orange juice and a croissant, perhaps lightly scrambled eggs on a square of whole-wheat toast and three pork sausages from Fortnum & Mason. This food was disgusting. Tad was sure he would only be able to manage a few mouthfuls and he was amazed to find himself eating it all. After that he drained a whole mug of tea and only felt a little queasy when he found a cigarette end nestling in the dregs at the bottom.

"Feeling better?" Eric Snarby asked.

"A bit." Tad had almost said "thank you" but stopped himself at the last minute. Doll Snarby shifted on her seat and the next moment there was an explosion as she let loose a jet of stale air. Tad was horrified but Eric just grinned.

"Whew!" he exclaimed. "That nearly put out my cigarette!"

Doll grunted with satisfaction. She wiped her mouth on the sleeve of her dress and stood up. "All right," she said. "Let's get to work."

"Work?" Tad blinked.

"Don't you start, Bob," Doll yelled, casually striking the back of Tad's head with her hand. "You pull your weight or you don't eat."

"Come on! Get off your backside." Eric slapped him again from the other direction. "Let's get down to business."

It turned out that the Snarbys ran the Lucky Numbers booth at the carnival and Tad spent the rest of the morning helping to rig it up. First there were the prizes to be set out: large stuffed gorillas hanging comically from one hand with a half-peeled banana in the other. Then the booth itself had to be washed down, the electric lightbulbs hung and a few loose planks of wood hammered into place. The work was easy enough—but not for Tad. He had never done anything like this before and found it almost impossible. He got a stiff neck from carrying the toys, a handful of splinters from washing the booth and had only managed two bangs with the hammer before he had hit his thumb and gone off howling. Eric Snarby watched him with disgust. At noon, he shook his head, rolled another cigarette and went back into the caravan. There he found Doll, reading *The Sun* and munching a bag of chocolate cookies.

"What is it?" Doll wasn't pleased to see him.

"It's the boy. Bob." Eric lit the cigarette and sucked in smoke. "There's something about 'im. 'E's not 'imself."

Doll blew her nose noisily, then looked around for a hand-kerchief. "Of course he's not himself!" she exclaimed. "What do you expect with 'alf a tube of airplane glue inside 'im!"

Eric Snarby nodded and bit his lip. He seemed about to go, but then he stopped and looked up and suddenly there was fear in his eyes. "What 'appens if Finn wants him again?" he asked.

"Finn." Now it was Doll's turn to go pale. Even as she spoke the word, she seemed to shrink into herself, her rolls of flesh quivering.

"Suppose Finn wants the boy?" Eric persisted.

Both the Snarbys were silent now. Eric's cigarette was so close to his lips that it was actually burning them, but he didn't seem to notice. Smoke crept up the side of his face like a scar. Doll Snarby was clutching the last chocolate cookie. Suddenly it exploded in her hand, showering her husband with crumbs.

"Bob'll be all right," she said. "Finn's not due back for a couple of days. By the time he gets here, Bob'll be fine." She took a deep breath and lashed out with one hand, catching her husband by the ear. As he squealed in pain, she drew him close. "Just keep 'im away from the glue," she hissed. "Elmer's, Duco, apoxy, the lot! And Finn won't notice a thing!"

The carnival was busy that night. The rain had stopped and the people had come out, milling around the stalls and lining up for the rides. By then, Tad had learned two things, over-hearing the conversation of the other booth owners.

First it was Friday. Less than twenty-four hours had passed since he had gone to bed at Snatchmore Hall as Thomas Arnold David Spencer. And second, the fairgrounds had been set up in a place called Crouch End, not too far from his parents' second London home. Tad could run away. Surely he would be able to find his way home.

But what would he do when he got there? If he knocked on the door, his parents wouldn't even open it—not to a scruffy, fair-haired kid who probably looked like he'd come to steal the silver. They might even set Vicious on him! The thought of the dalmatian with its razor-sharp teeth was enough to make Tad tremble. He had nothing to prove that he was telling the truth. He didn't even have his own voice!

The more he thought about it, the more he realized he had no choice but to stay where he was—at least for the time being. Perhaps when he woke up the next day, he would find he had switched back again. Perhaps Spurling would turn up in the Rolls-Royce and drive him home. Perhaps . . .

The truth was that Tad wasn't used to making decisions for himself. He didn't know what to do, and even if he had known, he would have been too afraid to try.

A movement caught his eye. Tad turned. And that was when he began to think he really had gone crazy.

There was a man standing on the other side of the carnival, partly hidden in the shadows. Or was it a man? He was less than four feet tall with hair reaching down to his shoulders. He had dark skin and wore a tunic that left his legs and arms bare. There were two streaks of blue paint on his cheekbones and a leather collar around his neck. He was an Indian, Tad realized. Some sort of pygmy.

The man was staring at Tad. Tad could see the lights of the carnival reflected in his dark eyes. Now he gestured with his head and walked slowly, deliberately, away. The message was clear. He wanted Tad to follow him.

Tad stepped forward, pushing through the crowd. He passed close to a hot-dog stand and caught the sweet, heavy smell of frying meat. The Indian had stepped out of sight and Tad quickened his pace, stepping over the cables and leaving the brightly lit center of the carnival. It was only now, in the darkness outside the ring of caravans, that he wondered if this was a good idea. Perhaps he was being led into some sort of trap. Perhaps the Indian had something to do with what had happened to him.

The chimes of the merry-go-rounds and the clatter of the other rides seemed suddenly very distant. The Indian had completely disappeared. Tad was about to turn around and go back when he noticed a vehicle that was set apart from the others. It was a real old-fashioned Gypsies' caravan, lavishly painted with silver and gold leaf. Above the door hung a sign:

DR. AFTEXCLUDOR
Your Future in the Stars

The Indian was standing in the doorway, three steps above ground level. He was lit now by a yellow glow that came from within. He nodded at Tad again, then turned and moved inside. Tad thought for a moment. Then he crossed the grass and gravel and walked up to the caravan.

The door was still open, but there was nobody in sight.

"Hello . . . ?" Tad called out.

Far away, the merry-go-round started up again. There was a snap and a clang from an air rifle aimed at a metal plate. A shout of laughter from the other side of the darkness.

Tad made his decision.

He climbed the three steps to the caravan door and went in.

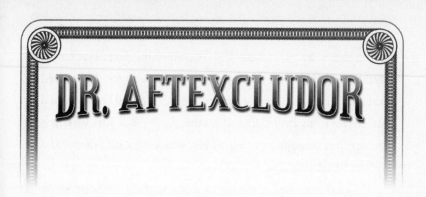

DR. AFTEXCLUDOR

It was like being inside some strange church or temple. Tad looked around, wondering just how much more could happen to him today.

The walls of the caravan were covered with thick material, like a tapestry. The floor was richly carpeted. Even the ceiling was hidden by folds of what looked like silk. There were no windows and hardly any furniture. Cushions were scattered on the carpet around a low wooden table on which stood a gleaming crystal ball. There were old leather-bound books piled up in crooked towers, but there were no shelves. Dozens of joss sticks poked out of strange bronze holders, their tips glowing, filling the room with smoke. The only other light came from a row of candles, perilously close to the wall. Sneeze and the whole place will go up in flames, Tad thought.

The owner of the caravan was sitting cross-legged on one of the cushions, smoking a long pipe. He was wearing a red silk dressing gown with a heavy collar and a strange black hat, a bit like a fez. The man had brown skin, deep black eyes and a pointed nose and chin. His hair was silver. Tad would have said he was about sixty or seventy. He had the look of a statue that has been left out in the open—not just weather-beaten but somehow timeless. His was a very odd face and a rather unsettling one.

"Good evening," the man said in a slightly singsong voice. "Would you mind closing the door?"

Tad did as he was told, instantly cutting out all the sounds of the carnival. The man waved a languid hand. "Please sit down."

Tad looked for a chair, couldn't see one, so sat down on a cushion. "Who are you?" he demanded.

"They call me Dr. Aftexcludor," the man said.

"Dr. Aftexcludor?" Tad thought for a moment. "That's a stupid name," he said. "I don't believe it's your real name at all."

The man sighed. "What are names?" he asked. "They're labels. Things people use to make us into what they want us to be." He fell silent for a moment. "And what of your name?" he demanded. "Bob Snarby." He spoke the two words with a smile.

"That's not my name!" Tad looked more closely at the old man. "But you know that, don't you. You know who I am!"

Dr. Aftexcludor nodded slowly. "Yes. I do know what has happened to you. At least, I think I can guess."

"What *has* happened to me? I insist that you tell me. If you don't tell me, I'm going to the police! It's horrible and unfair and I'm fed up with it. This carnival, the Snarbys, having to work! I want my mother. I want my Rolls-Royce. I want to go home!"

Dr. Aftexcludor chuckled. "Well, you certainly don't sound like Bob Snarby," he muttered.

Just then, a curtain parted and the Indian reappeared, holding a tray. Tad hadn't realized that the caravan had two sections, but looking over the Indian's shoulder, he saw what seemed to be a corridor extending some way into the distance. But that was impossible. The corridor was longer than the caravan itself. The curtain fell back and the Indian moved forward. On the tray were two steaming glasses of tea.

"I haven't introduced you," Dr. Aftexcludor said. "This is Solo."

"Solo?"

"That's not his real name either. I call him that because there's only one of him left."

"What do you mean?"

"He's from Brazil. An Arambaya Indian—but he's the last of the tribe. I met him in Rio de Janeiro and brought him with me to Europe . . ." Dr. Aftexcludor turned to the Indian and muttered a few words in a language that sounded a little like Spanish, a little like a dog barking. The Indian nodded and withdrew. "I won't tell you his story now," he said. "You're not ready for it."

31

"What do you mean?" Tad snapped. There was something about Dr. Aftexcludor he didn't like. Maybe it was that the old man seemed to know so much but explained so little.

Dr. Aftexcludor picked up his tea. "Perhaps we should begin with you," he said. "Tad Spencer. That's your real name, if I'm not mistaken."

"How do you know my name?" Tad demanded.

"It's my job!" The old man nodded at the table and for the first time Tad noticed the crystal ball. He looked into it and saw the inside of the caravan, the doctor, himself, all twisted into a swirl of colors, trapped inside the brilliant glass. "Your future in the stars," Dr. Aftexcludor explained. "Two dollars and fifty cents and I tell people everything they want to know. Although, of course, most people don't know what they want to know and what they do want to know isn't what they ought to want to know." He shook his head as if trying to make sense of this. "Anyway," he went on, "telling their name is the easy part."

"What's happened to me?" Tad demanded. He forced himself to look away from the crystal ball.

"That's not so easy. Obviously you've switched places with Bob Snarby—"

"You mean he's in my body with my parents in my house!" The thought hadn't occurred to Tad until this moment.

"I'm afraid so. But the real question is, how has this happened?" Dr. Aftexcludor smiled to himself and for just one moment Tad wondered if he knew more than he was letting

32

on. "I would say, if you want a professional opinion, that you've been hit by a wishing star."

"A what?"

"A wishing star. They're an extremely rare phenomenon and they have to be in exactly the right position at exactly the right time. Let me see . . ." Dr. Aftexcludor reached out and took one of the books. He opened it and Tad saw that it was an old book about astronomy, the heavy pages (handwritten, not printed) filled with diagrams of stars and planets and their possible alignments. "Yes. Here we are." He pointed to one of the pictures. "In the Andromeda galaxy. This little star here—Janus, its name is. That's Latin, although of course I wouldn't need to tell you that. Janus moved into the right orbit for about thirty seconds last night. That would have been around about ten o'clock. And the simple fact is that if you had made a wish at exactly that moment, the wish would have come true."

Tad stared at the picture, trying to think back. Then he remembered. "I wished I was somebody else," he said slowly.

"Well, there you are, then," Dr. Aftexcludor said. "That's just what you are. Somebody else. Perhaps you'd better have a sip of tea."

Tad blinked. "Wait a minute," he spluttered. "You're telling me . . . I wished. And my wish came true?"

"Evidently."

"But then . . . I can wish again! Why can't I wish myself back the way I was?"

"Well, of course you can," Dr. Aftexcludor said. "But the one snag is that you'll have to wait for the same star, Janus, to return to the same orbit."

"When's that?" Tad was excited now. For the first time he could see a way out of this nightmare.

Dr. Aftexcludor opened the book at another page and ran a long, skeletal finger down a column of figures. He flicked back a few pages, closed his eyes as he worked it all out, then slammed the book shut. "January thirteenth," he said.

"January thirteenth!" Tad almost burst into tears. "But that's seven months away!"

"Rather more, I'm afraid," Dr. Aftexcludor muttered. "I'm talking about January thirteenth in the year 3216."

"But that's . . . that's . . ."

"One thousand two hundred and twenty years from now. Yes. I know. You'll be one thousand two hundred and thirty-three years old."

And then Tad did begin to cry, more than he had ever cried in his life. Dr. Aftexcludor looked at him sadly. "I'm sure it's not that bad," he said.

"Of course it's bad!" Tad wailed. "It's terrible! It's the worst thing that's ever happened."

The doctor handed Tad a handkerchief and Tad blew his nose. "What am I going to do?" he asked miserably.

"I'm not sure there's anything you *can* do," Dr. Aftexcludor replied. "You are Bob Snarby now—whether you like it or not." He reached out and patted Tad on the shoulder. Tad looked up and once again he wondered if the old man wasn't hiding something. It was there in his eyes. Dr. Aftexcludor was doing his best to look sympathetic, but Tad knew that deep down he was enjoying this. "I can give you one bit of advice, though."

"What's that?"

"Well. I know it won't look that way at the moment, but perhaps you might end up actually enjoying being Bob Snarby. Or to put it another way, maybe you can do a better job of being Bob Snarby than Bob Snarby ever did."

"But I'm not Bob Snarby!"

"That's just my point."

Tad had had enough. He threw down the handkerchief and stood up. "I don't know what you're talking about," he said. "And I don't believe you anyway. I've never heard of wishing stars. I don't believe they exist. I think it's all just a lot of lies, and when I wake up tomorrow I'll be back to myself and that will be that. I'm not interested in you or your stupid servant. In fact I never want to see either of you again." Tad stormed out of the caravan, slamming the door behind him. Dr. Aftexcludor watched him go.

"Good-bye, Tad," he muttered. "Or should I say . . . hello, Bob?"

Tad spent the rest of the evening hiding and crept back into the Snarbys' caravan only when the carnival had closed for the night. He had begun to feel ill and wondered if he had caught a cold when he had been sent out, half naked, into the rain. One moment he was too hot, the next he was shivering with cold. There was a heavy thudding in his head.

Eric and Doll were not pleased to see him.

"Screwed off all afternoon, 'ave we?" Eric complained. "Where've you bin, then, Bob? 'Aving a bit of a laugh? Breaking into cars, I'll bet. Or vandalizing the elderly again."

"I've been thinking," Tad said. He coughed loudly and shivered again.

"Thinking? Thinking?" Both the Snarbys burst into malicious laughter. "You never done no thinking in your life," Doll exclaimed. She had been holding a cream éclair and now she took a huge bite. Cream oozed out of her hand. "You was bottom of the class in everything at school," she went on with her mouth full. "Bottom in math. Bottom in history. Second to bottom in geography—and that was only because you gave the other boy multiple stab wounds!"

"So what was you thinking about?" Eric Snarby asked. "Don't tell me!" He grinned. "It was Einstein's theory of electricity."

"It's relativity," Tad said. He found it hard to catch his breath. "Einstein invented the theory of relativity."

"Don't you contradict your father!" Doll exploded, grabbing hold of Tad's ear.

"That's right," Eric cried, grabbing hold of the other one.

"Wait a minute. Please. You don't understand . . ." Tad tried to get to his feet, but suddenly the caravan seemed to be moving. He felt it spin around, then dive as if down a steep hill. He flailed out, trying to keep his balance. Then fell unconscious to the floor.

There was a long silence.

"Blimey!" Doll said, looking at the silent boy. "That's a bit of a shocker! Is 'e dead?"

"I don't fink so," Eric Snarby muttered. He leaned down and put a hand to Tad's lips. "'E's still breathing. Just." He blinked nervously. "Wot we gonna do?" he went on. "I suppose we'd better call a doctor."

"No way! Forget it!" Doll snapped. "A doctor'll take one look at all them bruises we given the boy and then we'll have the social workers in and then the police."

Eric Snarby went over to an ashtray and rummaged inside it. A moment later he pulled out an old cigarette butt, relit it and screwed it into his lips. "So what are we going to do?" he asked again.

Doll Snarby thought for a long moment, twisting her wooden necklace with one pudgy hand. "We'll look after 'im ourselves," she said.

"But 'e looks awful!" Eric Snarby protested. "'E could be full of glue, Doll. Maybe 'is 'eart and lungs 'ave got all stuck together and that's wot's doing it. What are we going to do if 'e dies?"

"He won't die . . ."

"But what if 'e does? What will we tell Finn?"

At the mention of Finn, Doll froze. "Don't talk to me about Finn," she rasped.

Eric Snarby went over to Tad, picked him up and carried

37

him through to the bed. But for the faintest movement of the boy's chest as it rose and fell, he could have been dead already. Doll stared at him with bulging eyes, then threw a soiled blanket over him. "Go out and get 'im two Mars bars and a bottle of Gatorade," she rasped. "And don't worry! The boy's going to be fine!"

FINN

But Tad only got worse.

Wrapped in filthy sheets in the corner of the caravan, Tad seemed to be breathing more and more slowly, as if he had found the one sure way out of his new body and was determined to take it. Eric Snarby sat watching over him while, in the next room, Doll Snarby blinked back tears and tried on different hats for the funeral. But then, three days after Tad had fallen ill, there was a knock on the door. It was Solo, the Indian from Dr. Aftexcludor's caravan.

"Blimey!" Doll exclaimed, staring at the tiny figure. "It's the last of the blooming Mohicans. What do you want, dearie?"

By way of an answer, Solo held out a curious bottle. It was circular in shape, fastened with a silver stopper. It was half filled with some pale green liquid.

"What is it?" Doll demanded.

Eric Snarby appeared at the door beside her. "Don't touch it," he muttered. "It's some sort of foreign muck." He waved at Solo. "Beat it!" he shouted. "Go on! *Allez-vous!* Push off!"

"Medicine." Solo muttered the single word and nodded at the bottle.

"What do you know about medicine?" Eric sneered.

Doll snatched the bottle from him. "Shut up!" she exclaimed. "That old geezer 'e works for . . . Aftexcludor. 'E's a doctor, innee?"

"Medicine," Solo repeated.

"I 'eard! I 'eard!" Eric muttered sourly. He turned to Doll. "'Ow do they even know the boy's ill?" he whispered. "We didn't tell no one."

"What does it matter 'ow they knew?" Doll uncorked the bottle and smelled the contents. She wrinkled her nose. "It smells all right," she said. She nodded at Solo. "All right, you can shove off, shorty!" she said. "And tell your boss thanks, all right?"

Whether Solo had understood or not, he turned and walked away.

Doll turned to Eric. "Get me a glass!" she ordered. "And make sure you wipe it first with your sleeve."

Dr. Aftexcludor's medicine was the first liquid that Tad had accepted since he fell ill. Even the smell of it seemed to revive him a little and he emptied the glass in one swallow. After that he slept again, but his breathing seemed to have steadied and a little color crept back into his face. Then, that evening, quite suddenly he woke up. The fever had broken.

"My baby!" Doll threw her arms around Tad and burst into tears.

"Be careful!" Eric muttered. "You're so fat you'll smother 'im!"

Eric and Doll Snarby were so relieved to have their son back with them that later that evening they went out and bought fish-and-chips for him—although Doll Snarby ate most of the chips as she carried them home. That night Tad ate properly for the first time. And when he slept again, it was a normal, healthy sleep.

With the change in Tad's health came a change in the weather. The sun shone and the crowds came out, enjoying the first weeks of the summer holidays. When she was sure he wouldn't collapse on her, Doll Snarby set Tad to work on the Lucky Numbers booth.

It wasn't difficult to run. All Tad had to do was to sit in front of the stuffed gorillas holding a big basket of tickets. And as the crowds walked past, he would shout out a patter he had quickly learned from his new father.

"Come on! Try your luck! Three tickets for a buck. If it ends in a five, you're a winner! Lots of chances! Come on, sir! See if you can win a nice cuddly toy for the missus!"

This is what Tad did for the next four days. He felt safe in the booth, sitting on his own, and he even enjoyed the work, sitting out in the sun, watching the crowds go by. There was one thing that puzzled him to begin with. Not one single ticket that he sold actually ended in a five and soon he was surrounded by hundreds of colored scraps of paper—torn up and thrown away by the losers. The gorillas stayed where they were. But it didn't take him long to work out the answer. There *were* no fives. No fifty-fives, no sixty-fives, no hundred and fives. They had never even been printed. And the punters had as much chance of winning a cuddly toy for the missus as they did of waking up on the moon.

But Tad didn't mind. He didn't feel a twinge of guilt. Eric Snarby was giving him five cents out of every dollar he made and the money was quickly mounting up. Tad felt better with coins in his pocket. He felt more like his old self.

Before he knew it, he had settled into a routine. The fair closed just after midnight and Tad shut up the booth and crawled into his bed at the back of the caravan after quickly swallowing down a meal. The Snarbys bought him take-out Chinese, take-out Indian, take-out fish-and-chips. And the cost of each meal they took out of his earnings. Bed was the worst time for him. Lying curled up on the lumpy mattress, he would think back to his life at Snatchmore Hall. He had been away from home for just over a week, but somehow home had already become a distant memory. As he shivered in the damp air, Tad would remember his electric blanket, the chocolate that Mitzy placed on his pillow last thing at night, the Jacuzzi waiting for him in the morning. Could he go back? Tad doubted it. If he turned up at Snatchmore Hall looking the way he did now, talking the way he did, smelling the way he did . . . they wouldn't even let him through the gate.

"You are Bob Snarby now—whether you like it or not."

That was what Dr. Aftexcludor had told him and Tad believed him. He *was* Bob Snarby. He had no choice.

Another week passed and the fairgrounds prepared to close. Eric and Doll Snarby were planning to travel north to join another, larger carnival in Great Yarmouth. Tad had almost laughed when he heard that. Great Yarmouth was only forty miles from Snatchmore Hall. He was actually moving closer to home! But at the same time he knew that it might just as well have been four hundred miles for all the difference it would make.

He sold almost two hundred tickets on the last day. It was a weekday afternoon and he had been left on his own. Eric and Doll had opened a bottle of wine at lunchtime and had gone back to the caravan to sleep it off. He had watched the caravan shaking on its wheels and had heard their screams of laughter as they chased each other around the bedroom, but now it was silent and he imagined they were asleep. Tad picked up the bucket of tickets and shook them.

"Come on! Try your luck . . ." he began. Then stopped.

A man had limped up to the stall and was standing in front of him, looking at him strangely. Tad's first impression was of a shark in human form; the man had the same black eyes and pale, lifeless flesh. Although he wasn't physically huge, there was a presence about him, something cold and ugly that seemed to reach out and draw Tad helplessly toward him. The man had gray hair, cut short to match the gray stubble on his chin. He wore a shabby suit and a pair of perfectly round wire-frame spectacles.

And then he turned his head and Tad gasped. His face was normal on one side, but the other was completely covered by a tattoo. Somebody had cut an immense spiderweb into the man's white flesh. It stretched from his ear to his forehead to his nose, to the side of his mouth and down to his neck. The tattoo was livid black and—most horrible of all—it seemed to be eating its way into the man's flesh. Somehow it was almost more alive than the face on which it hung.

"Try your luck . . . ?" Tad muttered, but the rest of the words refused to come.

"Hello, Bobby-boy!" The man smiled wickedly, revealing a line of teeth riddled with silver fillings. He had more fillings in his mouth than teeth. "I hope you're well."

"I'm okay." Tad looked at the stranger warily.

"I asked if you was well," he said. "Are you one hundred percent? 'Okay' is not good enough!"

"I'm fine," Tad answered, mystified.

"That's good. Because I hear—I'm reliably informed—that you been ill," the man said.

"What about it?" Tad had learned that the ruder he was, the more people would accept that he was Bob.

The man smiled again. He had been leaning on a black, silver-capped walking stick, but now he leaned it against the stall. "Glue was what I heard," he murmured.

"What about it?"

The man shook his head slowly. "You modern kids," he

44

said. "When I was your age, you wouldn't have found me touching stuff like that. No. Gin was good enough for me. A half bottle of gin in my schoolbag, that's what got me through the day." He took out a cigarette and lit it. "Mind you," he went on, "gin could be a treacherous friend too. It's gin I got to thank for this . . ." He tapped the tattoo on the side of his face.

"What happened?" Tad asked, feeling queasy.

"I was drunk. Drunk as a lord. And some mates of mine took me down to the tattooist for a laugh. When I woke up, this was what he'd done to me. The web and the spider." Tad glanced at the tattoo. The man laughed. "One day I'll tell you where he put the spider," he said. He blew out smoke. His eyes behind the round lenses were suddenly distant. "Anyway, I had the last laugh, so to speak. I went back to the tattooist and gave 'im what you might call a piece of my mind."

"You told him what you thought of him . . ." Tad said.

"I *wrote* him what I thought of him. That's what I did. I tied him to a chair and wrote it all over his body. Used his own needles. Oh yes. I turned that man into a walking dictionary— and not the sort of words you'd want your mother to hear. He went nuts in the end, I understand. He's in an institute now. An institute for the insane. The other inmates never talk to him. But sometimes they . . . *read* him." The man broke off and laughed quietly to himself.

There was a commotion as the caravan door opened and Eric and Doll Snarby appeared, hurrying across the fairgrounds toward them. Eric was half dressed, his shirt out of his trousers and the sty under his eye throbbing in time with his breath. Doll was also a mess, her lipstick smeared and one earring missing. Tad had never seen them like this. They were, he realized, terrified.

"Finn!" Doll exploded. "What a pleasure to see you! What a joy!"

"We wasn't expecting you till later," Eric added. "Or naturally we would 'ave bin 'ere to welcome you."

"Please, my dear Snarbys!" The man called Finn positively beamed at them. "No need to get your underwear in a twist. I've had all the welcome I need, thank you." He nodded at Tad, and in that moment it was as if a conjuror had waved a silk scarf over the man's face. Suddenly the smile was gone and in its place was a leer of such force and ugliness that Tad shivered. "The boy's not 'imself," he snapped. "What have you done to 'im?"

"We looked after him!" Doll wheezed. "You know how precious he is to us, Finn. He was ill . . ."

". . . 'E made 'imself ill!" Eric interjected.

"What are children coming to?" Doll Snarby trilled. "You beat them senseless and it doesn't do any good at all! I don't know . . ."

"He got at the glue?" Each word was a bullet, fired at the Snarbys.

"It wasn't our fault, Finn!" Eric had gone chalk white.

"Oh Gawd! Please, Finn . . . !" Doll tried to slide herself behind her husband, but he pushed her away.

Finn thought for a moment. Then he relaxed and his face

rippled back to what it had been before. "I'm taking him with me this evening," he explained in a gentler voice. "A little business engagement. A business enterprise. I need my partner."

His partner? Tad heard the word and swallowed.

"Is he ready?" Finn asked.

"Of course he's ready, Finn," Doll croaked. "We wouldn't let you down!"

"That's settled, then," Finn said. "I'll be back for him at nine o'clock."

He picked up his stick and used it to unhook one of the gorillas. The gorilla slid down the length of the stick and into his hand. Finn smiled. "My lucky day!" he exclaimed. "It looks like I won!"

Holding the gorilla, he turned and limped away.

NIGHTINGALE SQUARE

There was a full moon that night. As Finn and Tad crossed the empty square, their shadows raced ahead of them as if searching for somewhere to hide. It was a few minutes after midnight. Tad had heard the church bells toll the hour. They had seemed far away, almost in another world. Here, everything was pale and gray, the buildings like paper cutouts against the black night sky.

Nightingale Square was in Mayfair, one of the trendiest areas of London. Tad had been here before and now recognized the square. Sir Hubert Spencer had friends here and had once brought Tad here for tea. Tad scanned the handsome Georgian houses with growing discomfort. He already had a nasty idea just what sort of "business" Finn had in mind. But what would he do if the chosen house was the very one where he had once been a guest?

Finn leaned against a metal railing in the middle of the

square and raised his stick. "That's the one," he whispered. "Number twenty-nine. That's my lucky number, Bobby-boy. It's the number of times what I been arrested."

Tad glanced at the house. It was tall and narrow with classical white pillars and wide marble steps leading up to the front door. It was on the corner of the square with an alleyway next to it leading, presumably, to a garden at the back. Thick ivy grew up one side of the house. Tad followed it with his eye. The ivy twisted past three windows and a balcony, stopping just short of the roof. At the very top there was a brightly colored box with a name and a telephone number. A burglar alarm.

"It's the London home of a real milord," Finn explained. "A member of the harry stocracy. 'Is name is Lord Roven."

At least it wasn't one of his father's friends. But Tad still couldn't relax. He listened with dread as Finn went on.

"I seen 'im in the papers, Bobby-boy. Lord Roven and his lovely wife, the two of them dripping with diamonds and gold and mink." Finn's eyes had gone dark now. A bead of sweat trickled down the side of his head. "It's not fair, is it?" he hissed. "Them so rich and us so poor. I never had no education, Bobby-boy. Okay. It's true. I did burn down the school. And maybe it was wrong of me to lock all the teachers inside it first. But I never 'ad a chance. Never! And that's why it's all right, you see. To break into 'is 'ouse and steal 'is things. Because he's got everything and we got nothing and stealing is the only way to make things change."

Breaking in. Stealing. Tad's worst fears had been realized.

His mouth had gone dry and it took him a few moments to find his voice. "How do you know Lord Roven won't be in?" he asked.

"'E always goes out tonight," Finn replied. "Tonight is 'is bridge night. It'll be four in the morning before 'e gets home."

"And Lady Roven?"

"In the country."

Finn licked his lips, then pointed again with the stick. "There's the window, Bobby-boy. Up there by the alarm. You can get in there."

Now Tad understood why he had been chosen. A man wouldn't have been able to climb up. The ivy wouldn't hold him. He needed a boy. "How do you know the window will be open, Finn?" he asked. His mind was desperately searching for a way out of this nightmare.

"I arranged it."

"But what about the alarm . . . ?"

The stick whistled down, missing Tad's head by less than an inch. "What's the matter with you?" Finn demanded.

"Nothing . . . !"

"Nuffing, Bobby-boy? Oh yes. There's something queer all right. Finn can smell a fish. A rotten fish." Finn rested the stick on Tad's shoulder and gazed into his eyes. "You been ill," he continued. "I can respect that. I've made lots of people ill my-self. But you're acting like you never been on a job before. What's happened to you?"

"I'm all right, Finn. Nothing's changed."

"I wonder." Finn let the stick slide off Tad's shoulder. "But you better not let me down, Bobby-boy. Stuffed with nice things this 'ouse is. Nice pictures and candlesticks. Smart jewelry and antiques. And you got to get me in!"

Finn looked left and right, then hurried across the road. Feeling sick and frightened, Tad followed. The last time he had come to Nightingale Square it had been for crumpets and tea. Now he was back as a thief in the night. It was impossible. When he had woken up in the Snarbys' caravan he had thought things were as bad as they could get. But this was far, far worse.

Finn had already reached the other side of the road and was crouching down. As Tad joined him, he straightened up and now he was holding what looked like a circular section of the pavement. Looking closer, Tad saw it was the cover of a manhole. Finn grunted and set it down, then pulled out a tangle of multicolored wires, which he began to examine.

"What are you doing?" Tad asked.

"What do you think I'm doing?" Finn shook his head and sighed. "The alarm's connected to the police." He pulled out a pair of wire cutters, selected an orange-colored wire and snipped it in two. "At least, it was."

"You've cut it!"

"Don't disappoint me, Bobby-boy." Finn glanced upward and suddenly it seemed to Tad that he was holding the wire cutters like a weapon. "You've seen it all before. You know the procedure. You know what's what."

"Of course, Finn."

"Good." Finn flipped the cutters over and put them away, then slid the manhole into place and stood up. "Fifteen minutes," he said. "That's how long we got before they'll send someone over to check." He gestured at the house. "I want the door open in five."

Tad stood staring at the house. A hundred excuses formed in his mind but died before they could reach his lips. He couldn't risk asking anything. Finn was already suspicious, and if Tad asked something he was supposed to know . . . he thought of the wire cutters and hurried forward.

Gingerly he reached out and took hold of the ivy, testing it against his weight. He had been right about one thing. The twisting stems would never have taken the weight of a man, but holding on tight he was able to lift himself off the ground. The ivy bent but held firm.

"Five minutes," Finn reminded him.

Tad began to scale the wall, pulling himself up a few inches at a time. Finn stood below, keeping a lookout along the empty pavement. Somewhere a car door slammed and an engine started up. Tad froze. But the sound grew more distant and finally disappeared. Tad grunted and dragged himself up over the first window.

He had passed the balcony and was making his way up to the third floor when he made the mistake of looking back down. It was the worst thing he could have done. The ground seemed a very long way away and for a moment he couldn't move. This sort of thing might have been easy for Bob Snarby, but Tad Spencer had always been afraid of heights. The whole

52

house had begun to spin with him attached to it and he was certain he would have to let go. Already he could imagine the wind sailing past him, the crushing impact as he hit the concrete below. He wanted to shout out, but he was too frightened even to draw breath.

There was a low whistle from the pavement. Finn. The sound snapped Tad out of his paralysis and he began to climb again. He was more afraid of Finn than he was of falling. It was as simple as that. He had to go on.

But the farther up he went, the thinner the ivy became. It was bending now, pulling away from the wall. Tad heard the unmistakable sound of a branch snapping and his left foot suddenly kicked out into space. For a ghastly moment he hung there, feeling himself topple backward away from the wall as the ivy came loose. Another branch broke. But then Tad lurched out and managed to grab a thicker clump. Carefully, he transferred his weight across. Then, gritting his teeth, he began to haul himself up farther.

He was only a foot from the window and was about to reach out to open it when there was a second low whistle—this time a warning. A moment later a car drove past, its headlights spilling out over the white front of the house. Instinctively, Tad stopped and pressed himself against the brickwork, not moving, not turning around. The car continued through the square and darkness fell like a curtain behind it. Finn whistled an "all clear." Tad began again.

He pressed his hand against the window and almost shouted with relief as it began to open inward. It wasn't locked! At least Finn had been right about that. The strange thing was that Tad wasn't frightened anymore. The truth was, he felt almost pleased with himself. At school he had never been any good at sports. He had never managed to get more than an inch or two up a rope and the parallel bars had made him feel sick. He had been excused from soccer and football—his parents thought they were too dangerous—and had even cheated at cross-country running by getting a taxi to wait for him around the first corner.

And now he had climbed fifty feet up the side of a building and he wasn't even out of breath! Tad didn't want to admit it, but it was true. He was proud of himself. He was pleased.

Letting go of the ivy with one hand, he reached out for the window. This was the difficult part, but he knew he had to keep moving. At least three minutes had passed since he had begun the climb. Finn had given him five. The police would be here in fifteen. Carefully, he swung his weight from the ivy onto the windowsill. Then he pulled himself up and in.

It was only at the very last moment that he lost his balance. Half in the house, half out of it, he suddenly found himself flailing at the air, his center of gravity hopelessly lost. Even then, some instinct saved him. He knew that he could topple backward and down or throw himself forward and in. He took the second option, twisted in midair and dived forward. His shoulders passed neatly through the window. Unable to stop himself, he pitched forward, then fell to the floor with a crash. The noise seemed deafening, but nobody came. Nobody had

heard. So Finn was right again. It seemed that there was nobody in the house.

The window had opened into a storage room, stacked high
with suitcases and tea chests. Tad could just make out a door
in the half-light and crept over to it. The door led out to a corridor with, straight ahead of him, a flight of stairs going down.
Tad tiptoed out.

Someone had left a light on in the hall. Tad hurried down
four flights of thickly carpeted stairs past paintings by Rubens
and Picasso. A huge chandelier hung over him and a gold-
framed mirror reflected his image as he scuttled over to the
front door. Tad was certain now that the house was empty. It
had that feel. His own feet rapped out a brittle sound on the
marble slabs in the hall. A grandfather clock ticked. But nothing else stirred.

He reached the front door and slid off the security chain
and drew back the bolts. The door opened and there was Finn,
standing in front of him, his glasses two brilliant white discs
as they caught the streetlight.

Finn lifted his walking stick and pushed Tad aside. He
hurried into the house and closed the door behind him.
There was a sheen of sweat on his forehead and a vein in his
neck was throbbing rapidly. The spiderweb was pulled taut.

"What the devil happened?" he hissed.

"What do you mean . . . ?" Tad began.

"You made the devil of a racket at the window, Bobby-boy.
An 'orrible racket. I'd have heard you three blocks away."

"I fell," Tad replied. "Anyway, what does it matter? The house is empty. You said so yourself."

Finn half smiled. "Got a tongue in your head, have you?" he snarled. "That sounds more like my old Bob." He glanced at his watch. "Seven minutes," he said. "We'd better move."

"Where are we going?"

"We'll start with the safe. On the second floor." Leaning on his stick, Finn hurried toward the stairs and began to climb. Tad followed, saying nothing.

They had reached the first landing when the door opened.

Finn saw it first and stopped. He was on a landing above, five steps below the level of the door, with Tad just behind him. A man in a blue silk dressing gown and leather slippers stepped out. He was in his sixties with silver hair and a gaunt face and Tad didn't need to ask his name. It had to be Lord Roven. The owner of the house was looking down at them, clutching a heavy silver candlestick as a weapon in his hand.

"Stop there!" he said in a cultivated voice. "I heard you come in the window and I've already called the police. You might as well wait where you are and make it easier on yourselves."

Finn looked over his shoulder at Tad and snarled at him with the cobwebbed side of his face. "You little fool!" he hissed. "You little idiot! I told you, didn't I? All that blooming noise!"

Tad took a step back. Everything was swimming again. He felt sick. He just wanted to disappear.

Finn turned back to Lord Roven. "What are you doing here?" he demanded. "Wednesdays is your bridge night."

Lord Roven frowned. He shook his head slowly. "It's Thursday . . ." he said.

"Thursday!" Finn almost shouted the word. A tic had appeared at one of his eyes, making the cobweb dance. "Thursday?" he whimpered again. "Then it's not my fault, is it? It was a perfect plan. Perfect! I just got the day wrong, that's all!"

Then everything seemed to collide with itself. Tad would never be quite sure what happened—or when.

The shrill sound of a siren cut through the night. Finn took a step forward. Lord Roven moved toward him, reaching out as if to grab him. Finn dropped his ebony walking stick—or part of it. When Tad looked again, he was still holding the handle, but the rest of the stick had fallen away and an ugly length of steel protruded from his hand. A sword stick, Tad realized. But Lord Roven hadn't seen it. Whether Finn lifted the sword or whether his victim walked onto it, Tad couldn't say. But the next thing he knew, Finn had laughed out loud, a single cry that danced in his throat. At the same time Lord Roven groaned and fell to the floor. Then there was a screech of tires. A blue light flashed on and off through a downstairs window. A hand hammered at the door.

"The kitchen!" Finn hissed, snatching up the rest of his walking stick. "We can get out the back way!"

"You've killed him!" Tad whispered.

Finn swore and then grabbed Tad by the throat. For a moment their faces were pressed so close that they touched and

Tad could feel the stubble of the man's beard rubbing against his own skin. "I'll kill you too if you don't move!" he snarled. "Now—come on!"

The thumping on the door continued, harder now, and a second police siren echoed across the square. Finn ran down the stairs—five steps at a time—and slid across the marble hallway. Tad followed. He could just make out a uniformed shape through the stained glass next to the front door, but he ignored it, twisting around to follow the passage back past the grandfather clock. Then Finn grabbed hold of him and pulled him through an open doorway even as a booted foot crashed into the front door, splintering the wood and smashing the first of the locks.

Tad found himself in the kitchen, a long, narrow room all white and silver with French windows leading into a garden at the end. Finn was already trying the handles, but they were securely locked.

"Stand back!" he ordered. As Tad obeyed, he raised his walking stick, then brought it whistling through the air into the glass. The window shattered at exactly the same moment as the front door was kicked in. Tad heard the falling wood, the sound of voices shouting in the hall. "Move!" Finn commanded.

Tad followed Finn into the garden. The lights on the police cars were still flashing and the bushes and trees loomed up on him, flickering blue against the night sky. The garden was surrounded by a low wall with other gardens on each side.

"Split up!" Finn hissed. "Confuse 'em. We got more chance

that way. Meet back at the caravan . . ." Then, before Tad could stop him, he hoisted himself over the wall and disappeared down the other side.

Tad swung around. Two policemen had stepped out of the kitchen and were standing in the garden. Slowly, they began to approach, and Tad realized they were afraid of him.

"All right . . ." one of them began.

Tad turned his back on them and ran. He felt his feet first on the grass, then in the soft earth of the flower beds. His scrabbling hands found the garden wall and he pulled himself up, half expecting the two policemen to grab him and pull him back. But he had been too fast for them. He twisted over the top of the wall and fell, squirming down the other side.

"There goes one of them! On the other side!"

A heap of garden rubbish had broken his fall. Tad stood up and brushed some of it away. There were more whistles, more shouts. Lights had gone on in the adjoining houses, illuminating the gardens that ran along the back. Tad looked one way, then another, then began to run. He reached another garden wall and threw himself over it. Then another. He had forgotten all about Finn, didn't care if he had been caught or not. Tad couldn't stop. A window opened in one of the houses and somebody shouted. He came to a garden fence, kicked out at it with his foot and broke through.

He found himself in a narrow alleyway. Down one end he could see flashing lights and hear voices. The other end was dark and silent. That was the direction he chose.

Tad never knew how he got away without being arrested.

But the alleyway led to a main road and suddenly he was in the clear with no policemen in sight and the chaos of Nightingale Square far behind him. He ran for an hour and only stopped when he could run no more.

He had escaped from Finn. He had escaped from the Snarbys. But now he was on his own and wanted for murder. He had little money, nowhere to go. Tad found an entrance to an office and slipped inside, burying himself in the shadows. He was still there six hours later when the first of the traffic hit the streets and the city of London woke to another day.

HOME

Bacon sandwich and a cup of tea, please."

Tad had found his way to a run-down café in a Soho back-street. He was the only customer. He paid for his breakfast using the last of his money and chose a table in the farthest corner. He had bought a late edition of the morning paper and now he opened it, thumbing through the pages.

He found the murder of Lord Roven in a single column on page four. There was a photograph of the house in Nightingale Square and a headline that read **BRUTAL MURDER IN LONDON'S MAYFAIR**. The report concluded that the police had chased two intruders, a man and a boy, but both had escaped. So Finn hadn't been arrested either! Tad didn't know whether to be pleased or sorry. If Finn was free, he couldn't lead the police to Tad. On the other hand, he would almost certainly be looking for Tad himself. After the disaster of the failed break-in,

Tad didn't like to think what would happen if he were found.

Tad bit into his sandwich and actually found himself enjoying it. He should have been terrified or in despair, but the truth was that he was neither. He felt confident . . . even calm. As he sat in the café with his elbows on the table and his long hair falling over his eyes, Tad wondered if he was changing in some way that he couldn't understand.

A couple more people came into the café and ordered coffees. Neither of them even glanced in his direction. Cupping his hands around his tea, feeling the warmth, Tad tried to work out his options.

He was a thirteen-year-old, on his own in London, wanted by the police. He knew that he had been seen at Lord Roven's house and it surely wouldn't be hard to track him down. And what then? The fact was that it had been Tad who had broken into the house and let Finn in. He was as responsible for the old man's death as if he had held the sword himself. If the police caught him, he would go to prison. It was as simple as that.

He had to get out of London. He knew that. But with no money in his pocket, it wasn't going to be easy.

Briefly, he considered going back to the carnival. Whatever he thought of them, Eric and Doll Snarby would look after him. And they'd take him with them when they moved to the carnival at Great Yarmouth. But if he went back to the Snarbys, he would be going back to Finn. Tad remembered the look on Finn's face as he stabbed forward with the sword. He shivered and took a sip of tea. He couldn't go back to Finn. There had to be another way.

And that was when the idea came to him.

Go home.

Not to the Snarbys but to his real parents and his own home. Sir Hubert Spencer had a house in Knightsbridge— only an hour's walk from where he was sitting now. It was his only chance. He had considered it before, when he was at the carnival at Crouch End. But things had been different then. He had been too frightened to think straight, too frightened to act. Tad had come a long way since then. He was certain now that he could make his parents believe what had happened to him. After all, he knew everything about them. He could describe things that only their true son would know. All he had to do was talk to them.

He finished his breakfast and set off, up through Green Park and on toward the heart of Knightsbridge. He followed the road past Harrods department store and thought sadly of the times he had visited it with his mother. Lady Geranium used to take him there on his birthday and let him choose his own present. One year it had been a grand piano (although he had never played it). The next he had chosen the entire chocolate department. But now, of course, they wouldn't even have allowed him through the door.

The Spencers' London home was in a quiet street on the other side of Harrods. Number One Wiernotta Mews was a pale blue house on three floors with a kitchen and dining room in the basement. Tad had a bedroom on the first floor and slept there whenever the family was visiting London. He wondered if they would be there now.

It was eleven o'clock and the mews was empty. The other home owners were probably all at work. Tad crossed the cobbled surface and reached for the bell. It was only then that he had second thoughts. If the Spencers were at home and he rang the bell, Spurling would probably come to the door. And what would the chauffeur see? A dirty, disheveled boy whom he wouldn't recognize. The door would be slammed before Tad had a chance to explain.

Tad sighed. It would be much easier to explain things once he was *inside* the house. But how was he to get in? Break in—for the second time in twenty-four hours? Then he remembered. His mother always left a spare key in one of the baskets of flowers that hung on either side of the front door. Tad quickly found it, opened the gate and followed the metal stairway down to the kitchen entrance.

As quietly as he could, he slipped the key into the lock and turned it. The house was silent. Tad stepped inside.

He stood for a few seconds in the quarry-tiled kitchen. His heart was pounding in his chest and he had to remind himself that he wasn't a thief. He wasn't breaking in. This was his house. He lived here. Even so, when he moved forward it was on tiptoe and his ears were pricked for the slightest sound.

He passed through the kitchen and crept upstairs. The first floor consisted of a single open-plan room with leather sofas, Turkish carpets and a huge wide-screen TV. A spiral staircase led upward and he followed it to the second floor, where his own bedroom was located. He stopped in front of a door, tapped gently and went in.

The room was just as he had left it—evidently nobody had been there in the last few days. His bed, with its quilt patterned like a giant dollar bill, was freshly made. His London toys, books and computers were exactly where he had left them. Tad ran his hand over one of the surfaces, taking it all in. He had come home! Quickly he stripped off his clothes and went through into the adjoining bathroom. He didn't care if anyone heard him now. He turned on the shower and stood for ten minutes in the hot, jetting water. It was as if the shower were washing away not just the dirt but all the memories of the past week. He dried himself in one of his own American towels. He had never appreciated how soft and warm they really were.

Outside, he heard a car pull up. A door slammed and a voice called out. He recognized it at once. It was his mother! His parents had arrived.

He felt a surge of excitement. In just a few moments he would see them again, talk to them, tell them what had happened. They would be shocked, of course. But once they understood, they could all begin again. The nightmare would finally be over.

Moving quickly, Tad pulled some clothes out of the closet and tried to get dressed. It was only now that he realized he had a problem. The boxers he was holding were obviously several sizes too big. The pants were the same. Reluctantly, he picked up Bob Snarby's clothes and put them back on. At least they fit, and washed and groomed, he felt a bit more like an ordinary boy, less like a street urchin. Even so he was nervous. What if his parents refused to listen to him? What if they simply threw him back out on the street?

He could hear footsteps coming up the stairs. Tad thought for a moment, then went over to a drawer beside the bed, opened it and pulled out a checkbook. It was his own checkbook, and he was certain that he would still be able to sign Tad Spencer's signature. There was over ten thousand dollars in his current account; his pocket money for the past six months. Whatever happened, that money was now his.

He had just shoved the checkbook into his pocket when the door to the bedroom opened. Tad stared. He wasn't sure what he had been expecting, but whatever it was, it certainly wasn't this.

A short, fat, dark-haired boy in a ginger-and-brown-checked suit had just walked in and was staring at Tad with the same shocked expression with which Tad was staring at him. Tad tried to speak. He felt the bed pressing against the back of his legs and he sat down. The other boy smiled.

And that was when Tad knew. He had thought at first that he was looking at himself, and in a way, of course, he was. It *was* his own body that had just walked into the room, but there was somebody else inside it. And the suddenly narrowed eyes—the cruel smile—told him who that somebody was.

"Bob Snarby!" he whispered.

"Tad Spencer!" the other boy replied. "I been expecting you."

FACE-TO-FACE

Bob Snarby closed the door and moved into the room. Tad watched him with a sense of wonderment. His first thought was how fat this boy was, how arrogant he looked with his puffed-out cheeks and slicked-back hair. But then he remembered that he was actually looking at himself! Bob was wearing one of his own favorite suits. The Rolex watch that his mother had bought him was on the other boy's wrist. Tad realized that he was jealous, that he disliked Bob Snarby on sight.

But it wasn't Bob Snarby. It was him! Tad rested against a chair, thoroughly confused.

For a long minute the two boys stared at each other; Bob Snarby in Tad's body and Tad Spencer in Bob's body. At last Tad spoke.

"Do I call you Bob or Tad?" he asked.

The fat boy smiled. "I suppose you can call me Bob," he said. "You know that's who I am."

"What happened?" Tad demanded. "How did you turn yourself into me?"

"I didn't," Bob replied. "I didn't have nothing to do with it."

"You're lying!"

Bob moved farther into the room. "I'll tell you what happened," he said. "But you'd better not get nasty with me. Spurling's downstairs and one shout from me and you'll be out on your ear. Know what I mean?"

Tad nodded.

"All right." Bob sat down on the bed. "I'd had an 'orrible day at the carnival. Up in Crouch End. Moving in is always the worst part and I was dog tired . . . only if I was a dog they'd 'ave put me out of my misery. Mum and Dad were out at the pub. I went to bed."

"What time?"

"It must have been about ten-thirty. Anyway, I fell asleep and woke up in your place. That's all there was to it. One minute I was in the van, the next . . ." Bob shook his head. "It gave me a nasty shock, I can tell you. Waking up in that bed! It was so big it took me a while just to find my way out."

"So what did you do?" Tad asked.

"I couldn't believe it at first. There I was, surrounded by all this gear—CDs and computer games and the rest of it. You know what my first thought was?"

"I can guess," Tad said.

"Bob, my boy, I thought, you've got to steal as much of this stuff as you can carry. You can ask questions later. But right now you've got to get out of here before someone comes and throws you out." Bob sighed. "That was when I caught sight of meself in the mirror." He paused. "I mean, *my*self, don't I. I've got to learn how to talk proper, haven't I! Anyway, that was when I started screaming the place down. It was like a horrible dream—only I knew I was awake."

"That's more or less what happened to me," Tad muttered.

"I bet. You must have been sick waking up with Eric and Doll! I wish I could have seen your face!"

"You've got my face!" Tad retorted angrily.

"Let's not make it any more confused, shall we?" Bob Snarby said. "Where was I? Oh—right. I'm screaming my head off when the door flies open and this old biddy comes rushing in. I didn't know who the hell she was, but then she starts calling me 'Master Tad' and tries to get me to calm down . . ."

"It was Mrs. O'Blimey," Tad said.

"That's right. The housekeeper. Well, I got back into bed and the old lady fussed over me, but I kept my mouth shut. You see, I knew something strange was going on and I didn't want to screw things up, like. You know? I could smell the money and I was thinking to myself—Bob, old buddy, I don't know what's going on 'ere. It's a right mystery and no mistake.

But you could do yourself quite nicely out of all this. Just take your time. Try and work it all out . . ."

Bob Snarby pulled a bar of chocolate out of his pocket and broke a piece off. "I never used to like this stuff," he said, half to himself. He offered the bar to Tad. "You want some?"

Tad shook his head.

"Well, I did manage to work it out in the end," Bob continued, munching the chocolate. "Somehow—Gawd knows how—I'd switched bodies with a fat, rich boy called Tad Spencer. It was like something out of a comic. Or maybe a film. I once saw a film on TV where something like that happened. I don't know. Anyway, as I lay there in that great big bed, surrounded by all that lovely stuff, I realized it had happened to me and after a bit I stopped worrying about how or why and just decided to . . . go with it."

"But how could you persuade them?" Tad thought back to his own experiences with the Snarbys and with Finn. "My mother and father would never have believed you were me. You're much too common. You don't know anything. You never been to private school."

"You mean—'You never *went* to private school,'" Bob corrected him. "It's true what you're saying, although if you don't mind me saying so, Tad, you're not exactly in a position to be snobbish." He smiled. "But all right, I admit it. There were a lot of things I didn't know that I ought to if I really was going to be you. I knew that."

"So what did you do?"

"In the end it was easy. I hadn't said much yet, so they didn't know anything was wrong. The old woman—Mrs. O'Blimey—thought I'd just been having a bad dream. And that afternoon, Spurling asked me if I'd like to go out riding. I said yes—I thought he was talking motorbikes or something. I didn't realize he meant on a horse! No, thank you very much, I thought. But then, as I said, I had this idea. I got on the horse and the two of us trotted along for a bit. And then I fell off." Bob rubbed his backside. "I didn't have to fake that bit, I can tell you. Your mum saw me fall. She had the horse shot immediately—but this is the good part." He winked at Tad. "I told her I'd banged my head when I fell and I wasn't seeing things straight. You know . . . like I had amnesia or something."

"Amnesia . . ." Tad almost admired Bob despite himself. The idea couldn't have been simpler.

"Right." Bob broke off another piece of chocolate. "Well, of course your mum was worried sick. She called in a whole army of doctors and I told them I wasn't sure who I was and that I'd forgotten all my Ancient Greek and Latin and all that stuff and they said that I definitely had a concussion. I had to stay in bed while they did all these tests and they only let me out a couple of days ago. Now your mum—or I should say my mum—has brought me down to London to go shopping. We're going on vacation in a couple of weeks . . ."

"A safari in Africa," Tad said gloomily.

"That's right! First-class flight. Five-star hotel. It's like winning the friggin' lottery!" He finished the chocolate and dropped the wrapper on the floor. "How about you?" he asked. "What do Eric and Doll have to say about the new Bob Snarby?"

"They think I've been sniffing glue," Tad said.

Bob thought about this for a moment, then threw his head back and laughed. "I bet they have!" he said. "Yeah. That'd explain everything."

Tad moved closer to the bed. "Listen to me, Bob," he pleaded. "We've got to straighten this out . . ."

"What do you mean?"

"We've got to tell them what's happened. Your parents and my parents. If we both tell them, they'll have to believe us and maybe they'll be able to find a way to turn us back into ourselves."

Bob stared at Tad as though he were mad. "But why should I want to do that?" he demanded.

"What?" Tad felt something cold reach out and touch the back of his neck.

"Why should I want to change back?" Bob said.

"Because you've got to!" Tad cried. "I can't be you and you can't be me. We've got our own parents and our own lives. We've got to put things back the way they were."

"Forget it!" Bob exclaimed. "I'm better off now than I've ever been in my entire life, and if you imagine I'm going to let you spoil it, you've got another think coming."

"It's all wrong . . . !" Tad began.

"It's perfect!" Bob shouted the words. "I never had a chance. I never had anything. Not from the day I was born.

73

Eric and Doll, they made me what I was and I was stuck with it. And do you know what made it worse? All around me, in the newspapers, on TV, in the stores, I saw all the things I could never, ever have. Computer games and iPods. Fancy clothes. TVs and videos. I'd never have them—not in my whole life—just because of who I was . . ."

"That's not true—"

"It is true! But you wouldn't understand that. You had it all, didn't you. It was all just given to you on a plate. Yeah— well, now you're finding out what it's like on the other side of the fence and I'm not surprised you want to switch back again. Only you can't. Because I won't let you."

"You have to!"

"I won't!"

Something inside Tad snapped, and before he knew what he was doing, he had thrown himself on top of Bob Snarby, his fists flailing, his face twisted with anger and hatred. He expected the other boy to defend himself, but Bob just fell back onto the bed with Tad on top of him, not even trying to push him off. Tad hit him, again and again, but his fists seemed to make no impact, slapping against the skin and sinking into the soft folds of flesh. He only realized now that Bob was shouting, calling for help. Suddenly the door crashed open. Out of the corner of his eye Tad saw a great bulk in a blue-and-gray uniform descending on him. Two hands reached out and grabbed him; one around his neck, the other under his arm. He was pulled off Bob and into the air as easily as if he were nothing more than a set of empty clothes.

"Are you all right, Master Tad . . . ?"

"Yes, Spurling. Thank you." Bob got unsteadily to his feet. His shirt was rumpled and there were tears welling up in his eyes.

"Spurling . . ." Tad twisted around in midair, his feet six inches off the ground. As much as he squirmed and struggled, he couldn't free himself from the chauffeur's grip.

"Who are you?" Spurling demanded. "What are you doing here?"

Tad opened his mouth to answer, but before he could speak, before he could find the right words, Bob moved forward. "He was here when I came in," he sobbed. "He was searching the room. I think he was looking for something to steal."

"Tad, darling?" The voice came from outside the room and the next moment Lady Geranium Spencer appeared. She took one look at Tad and her face paled. "How frightful!" she exclaimed. "It's a burglar!"

"Mummy . . . !" Bob Snarby ran into Lady Geranium's arms. "He attacked me!" he wailed.

"Spurling! Call the police immediately," Lady Geranium snapped. She pushed Bob away from her. "Do be careful, darling," she continued. "You're going to rumple Mummy's hair."

"Wait a minute!" Tad shouted. "You're not his mother! You're *my* mother!"

"I'm nothing of the sort!" Lady Geranium replied. "Oh, Spurling! Take him downstairs. I think I'm going to have one of my headaches."

"Yes, ma'am."

Tad opened his mouth to speak again, but Spurling shook him so hard that all the breath went out of him. There was nothing he could do as he was carried out of the room, half across the chauffeur's massive shoulders.

Spurling carried Tad back downstairs, threw him into a closet and locked the door. Suddenly everything was black, apart from a tiny chink of light coming through the keyhole. Tad pounded at the door, then, realizing it was useless, sank to his knees. He heard something outside. He pressed one eye against the keyhole. Spurling was on the telephone, waiting to be connected. There was a movement and Lady Geranium appeared, hand in hand with the boy she thought was her son.

"We're going out, Spurling," she snapped.

"Yes, ma'am."

"Come along, Tad!"

Inside the closet, the real Tad watched Bob Snarby turn around and gaze directly at him. Bob's lips twisted in a cruel, triumphant smile.

And then he was gone.

ACID

The office was small and square with a desk, two chairs, a filing cabinet and a low coffee table. There was no carpet. A single window looked out over a tangle of railway lines with King's Cross Station in the far distance. Tad was sitting on his own. He had been here now for twenty minutes, but he still had no idea where he actually was.

After Bob Snarby had left with his mother, Spurling had unlocked the closet door. Of course Tad had tried to speak, to explain who he was, but after just two words the chauffeur had cut him off.

"You don't talk to me. I don't want to know. Keep your mouth shut—or else!"

Tad had known Spurling all his life. Only two weeks before, the man had been picking him up at school, carrying his suitcases for him. But it was a completely different creature who had pulled him out of the closet and who towered over him now. Behind the fancy uniform, the brightly polished buttons and the chauffeur's cap, the man was a thug. He had the same lifeless eyes as Finn. Tad didn't try to speak again. But he found himself wondering what such a man was doing working for his father.

With his arm twisted painfully behind him, Tad had been led out of the house and thrown into the back of a black Volkswagen station wagon. It must have been Spurling's own car. Tad had never seen it before. They had driven in silence for about half an hour, passing King's Cross Station. Then Spurling had suddenly swerved off the road, through an archway and into the parking lot of an office building. Tad hadn't had time to see what the building was. They had gone in through a side door, up two flights of stairs. Tad had glimpsed one large room, full of people talking on telephones, tapping at computers, shuffling papers among themselves. But the chauffeur had led him away from there, along a corridor and into the room where he found himself now. As soon as Spurling had gone, Tad had tried the door. It was locked.

He wasn't in a police station. At least, he didn't think so. There had been no police cars near the building and anyway it didn't have that sort of smell. But if it wasn't a police station, what was it? Tad looked around, searching for clues.

The desk and the filing cabinet were locked, like the door, and told him nothing. There were two posters on the wall. One showed a syringe with the line SAY NO TO DRUGS. The other was an advertisement for Crime Stoppers. Tad gazed out of the window as a train trundled past. King's Cross . . . somehow that meant something to him but he couldn't remember what.

Then there was the click of a key turning in a lock. The door opened and a young woman came in, carrying a file.

"Hello," she said. "My name is Marion Thorn. Please sit down."

As Tad moved away from the window, he examined the new arrival. Marion Thorn was tall and slender with long black hair and dark skin. She was wearing a gray jacket and pants with a brooch, her only jewelry, pinned at the lapel. Her manner was businesslike, but she had a pleasant smile with the perfect white teeth of a movie star.

Growing more puzzled by the minute, Tad sat down.

"I imagine you're wondering who I am," Marion said. "The first thing is to assure you—I'm not the police."

Tad was relieved but said nothing.

"What's your name?" Marion asked.

Tad thought for a moment. "Bob Snarby," he said.

"Bob Snarby." Marion opened the file and wrote the name down. "You do realize," she went on, "that Sir Hubert Spencer could have pressed charges. Breaking into his house, attacking his son . . . these are very serious offenses."

"It wasn't like that—" Tad began.

Marion held up a hand. "You're very lucky, Bob. Sir Hubert is a very unusual man. A very kind man. He's dedicated a lot of his life to helping young people like you. That's why he decided to send you over to us."

"Us . . . ?" But suddenly Tad knew where he was. Suddenly it all made sense.

"This office belongs to a charity," Marion explained. "We're called ACID."

"The Association for Children in Distress," Tad muttered.

"You've read about us?" Marion asked.

Tad almost wanted to laugh. How could he tell her that he had known about ACID all his life? "I read about you in the papers," he said.

Marion Thorn nodded. "ACID was founded by Sir Hubert Spencer," she explained. "We have a terrible situation in London. Children . . . out on the streets, some of them as young as eleven and twelve. They have nowhere to go. And there are terrible temptations." She nodded in the direction of the poster. "Drugs. Crime. And nobody cares about them. Nobody wants to know."

She paused and Tad was amazed to see real tears in her eyes. Marion took out a handkerchief and blew her nose. "We go out and find these children," she said. "We search the railway stations, the backstreets, the video-game arcades . . . and we bring them in. We help them and we want to help you, Bob. But first we have to ask you some questions. Do you mind?"

Tad shook his head. "Go ahead . . ."

Suddenly Marion Thorn was businesslike again. She spread the file on the desk and sat with pen poised. "How old are you?" she asked.

"Thirteen."

"How long have you been in London?"

"A couple of weeks."

"Are you homeless?"

"Yes." Tad hesitated. He didn't want to lie, but there was no way he could tell the whole truth. "I ran away from home."

"Your mum and dad must be very worried about you." Marion's voice was reproachful now.

"They don't care about me," Tad replied. "I bet they haven't told anyone I'm missing."

"Can you give me their address?"

"They don't have an address. They live in a caravan. They were in Crouch End when I left, but they could be anywhere now. I think they've gone north."

"So nobody knows where you are. You have no friends or relatives? No social workers? Nobody to look after you?"

"I'm all on my own," Tad said, feeling miserable.

"Good! Good!" Marion muttered.

Tad glanced at her. There was something in her voice that hadn't been there before. She sounded almost hungry. And her face seemed to have changed too. Her dark eyes were gleaming as she made a hurried note at the bottom of the file. She looked up and saw Tad staring at her. At once she relaxed. "What I mean is . . . it's good that we found you," she explained. "ACID is always interested in young people with no families. That's where we do our best work."

"What exactly do you have in mind?" Tad asked.

Marion glanced at him curiously, as if there was something about him that didn't quite add up. But whatever was in her mind, she dismissed it. "All we want to do is to get you off the street," she said. "That means somewhere to live, a good meal inside you and a chance to earn some money to support yourself. ACID has a center just outside London where we run education programs for boys like you. That's what it's called . . . the Center. I'd like to take you there now."

For some reason that he couldn't understand, Tad was uneasy. Perhaps it was the look he had seen in Marion's eyes a moment before. "What if I don't want to go?" he asked.

And there it was again. A sudden hardness behind that smiling, beautiful face. "Then we'd have no choice but to hand you over to the police, Bob. The break-in at Sir Hubert's was a very serious matter. I'm afraid it's us or it's prison."

Tad considered. Marion reached out and clasped his hand. Her fingers were long, her nails perfect. "We only want to help, Bob," she said. "Have you got anywhere else to go?"

And suddenly Tad was angry with himself. This was his parents' charity! What was there to worry about? For the first time since the switch had taken place, someone was actually trying to help him, and instead of being grateful, he was almost being rude. He sighed. "I haven't got anywhere else to go," he said. "And I'm glad I was brought to you. You can take me to the Center."

Marion smiled. She closed the file. "Good," she said. "We'll leave at once."

There was a black van waiting for Tad in the lot behind the building. As he walked across the blacktop toward it, he felt a sudden chill. The evening was drawing in, but it was still warm, and he paused, wondering what was wrong. Marion Thorn was next to him and she rested a hand on his arm. "It takes half an hour to get to the Center," she said. "You can sit in the back."

Tad looked at the van. It had no windows in the back, not even a small panel set in the door. It didn't have any logo on the side either. Its color made him think of a hearse.

"Is something wrong, Bob?"

Tad remembered the moment in the office, the chill in Marion's eyes. Then he dismissed it. ACID was his parents' charity. ACID was going to look after him. "No. I'm fine."

He got into the van. There was a bench along one side, metal with no cushions. A sheet of metal separated the back from the driving compartment. When Marion closed the door, Tad found himself entombed in a metal box that would have been pitch-black but for a single bulb burning behind a metal grille in the ceiling. He heard Marion walk around the side. A driver must have shown up, for there was a brief exchange. Two doors slammed shut and the engine started.

It was only then that Tad realized that—apart from Marion—nobody had seen him since he had left the Knightsbridge house. He had seen nobody. If anybody came searching for him now, it would be as if he had vanished off the face of the earth.

He had put himself completely in the power of ACID and its staff. As the van moved off, picking up speed, Tad wondered if he hadn't made a terrible mistake. ACID was a charity. ACID wanted to help him. Everything was going to be all right. Tad sat back and waited for them to arrive.

THE CENTER

Tad, washed and dressed in pale blue dungarees that reminded him uncomfortably of a prison uniform, followed Marion Thorn down a seemingly endless corridor, lit by a line of tiny halogen lights. Video surveillance cameras swiveled to follow them as they walked and a hidden air-conditioning system whispered all around them. Tad glanced through a large plate-glass window where test tubes and bottles, glass pipes and burners fought for desk space with computers and CDs and machines so complicated that he could only guess at their use. A man and a woman, both in white coats, came down the corridor the other way and passed them without speaking. Somewhere an intercom called out: "Dr. Eastman to room 113, please. Dr. Eastman to room 113."

He had barely glimpsed the Center as he had been led out of the van and into the nearest building. From the outside it looked like an ordinary industrial park: a cluster of dull redbrick buildings with frosted-glass windows allowing no view in or out. True, it was surrounded by a high wire fence with an electric security barrier permanently manned by a uniformed guard. But there was nothing unusual about that. People who lived nearby (and the Center was surrounded by ordinary houses) probably thought it was a small factory. If they ever thought about it at all.

Marion Thorn had reached a door and was punching in a combination number on the electronic panel next to it. Tad stopped. "Where are we?" he demanded. "What's going on?"

There was a buzz and the door clicked open. "In here, please, Bob," she said.

The room was a doctor's office. If Tad had been uneasy before, he was now positively alarmed. But, following Marion's pointing hand, he sat down on a narrow bed. A second door opened and two men came in. Both were short and round with curly black hair and wide, loose mouths. Both were bearded. It took Tad a second to realize that they were identical twins. He grimaced, wondering if he were dreaming. Tweedledum and Tweedledee in white coats with stethoscopes! What next?

That question was soon answered as the two men began a medical examination that started at Tad's head and went inch by inch all the way to his toes. The doctors—if that's what they were—seemed particularly interested in his hair, his teeth, his eyes and his skin.

"Excellent condition."

"Unusually good. Yes. Good dermatology . . ."

"Yes . . ."

They spoke to each other in short, clipped sentences. But never did they say a word to Tad. Lying on the bed, he felt like a piece of meat in a butcher's shop and he was relieved when it was finally over.

One of the doctors nodded at Marion. "You can take him down."

"Down where?" Tad demanded. He was angry now.

"This way, Bob." Marion opened the door.

Tad didn't speak as Marion led him back down the corridor to a wide area with a series of elevators. Various thoughts were turning over in his mind and none of them were very pleasant. If ACID really wanted to help him, they had an odd way of going about it. He wondered if his father had any idea what went on in the Center. This place was beginning to turn his stomach—and he decided to get out the first moment he could.

The elevator arrived and he and Marion got in.

"Up?" Tad asked.

"Down," Marion replied. Tad glanced at the panel beside the door. The elevator didn't have any buttons. The doors closed and it began to descend as if it had a mind of its own.

"Where are we going, exactly?" Tad demanded.

"You'll find out, Bob." Marion's voice was as calm as ever. "We're going to help you. But first we want you to help us . . ."

The elevator stopped. The doors opened. Tad stepped out and stared.

He was in a huge, vaulted chamber. It could have been an underground health club, a hospital or a television studio . . . His first impressions were of all three. First there were the showers and baths with steam rising into the air. Then there were what looked to be orderlies, doctors and scientists, dressed in white, bustling about with trolleys piled high with bottles, basins, bandages and the occasional syringe. And finally there were the television monitors flickering on steel gantries and, high overhead, the banks of brilliant arc lamps, flooding the scene with a harsh, unnatural light.

And then he noticed the other children.

Marion Thorn had told him that ACID collected children off the streets of London. What she hadn't told him was what happened to them next.

One boy was dressed only in swimming trunks, standing in an elaborate shower cubicle. The floor was slowly turning, and as the boy rotated he was sprayed by different-colored jets of water. An elderly woman was watching him closely and every few minutes she took a Polaroid photograph, clipping the results to a wall chart nearby.

Opposite him, a black youth of about eighteen was lying on a bed, completely covered in some sort of pale silver grease. The grease started at his ankles and went all the way to his neck. His eyes were hidden behind a large pair of goggles, obviously designed to protect him from the glowing neon tubes that hung only inches from his skin. Two men in white coats were watching him. Tad recognized the twins who had just examined him.

There were girls there as well. One was strapped to a high-backed chair, her feet immersed in a large bucket that buzzed and vibrated beneath her. A few yards away from her, a second had been hung upside down with wires attached to her ears and nose. Opposite her, in a partly screened-off area, another boy was being slowly spun in what looked like a giant washing machine, while next to him a girl of about twenty sat in a bath, with green foam bubbling around her neck.

Laboratory rats!

Tad felt something—a shiver or a scream—rising to his throat and had to force himself to hold it back. He'd never seen anything like it in his life. He'd had no idea what experiments were being conducted in this dreadful, secret place. But they were being conducted on children.

How had it happened? Somebody must have taken over ACID and twisted it to their own evil purposes. Even as he stared at the incredible activity all around him, Tad knew that he had to get out of there. He had to let his father know what was happening. Sir Hubert Spencer had powerful friends. Once he knew the truth, he would put an end to it.

A hand clamped down on Tad's arm and he looked up to see a blank-faced man dressed as a security guard. "This way," the man said in a voice that didn't allow for argument.

"Wait a minute—" Tad began.

But then Marion Thorn was at his side. "Don't worry, Bob," she said. "We're not going to hurt you—"

"What's going on here?" Tad began to struggle. The security man's grip tightened.

"It's just tests," Marion explained. "On your hair. On your skin. Your nails and your eyes. You did say you wanted to help us, Bob."

"But I didn't mean—"

Marion nodded at the security guard. "Take him to Area Seven."

Before Tad could say another word, the guard had jerked him forward, dragging him by the shoulder. Tad was shouting now, using words that he didn't even know he knew. Even then, as he was pulled farther into the chamber, he realized that he didn't only look like Bob Snarby: he was beginning to sound like him too.

"Prepare experimental Area Seven!" This voice came from a set of hidden loudspeakers and boomed in the air. Tad tried to dig his heels in. He passed a boy, lying asleep on a bed. The boy's hair had gone a brilliant shade of pink. Two more men were seeing to a second boy, helping him out of the washing machine.

"Amazing! He's been washed twenty-six times . . ."

"Yes. And he's hardly wrinkled at all!"

Tad yelled and dug his heels in. The security guard dragged him toward an empty bed.

Before he could do anything about it, he found himself thrown onto his back and firmly tied down with three straps over his neck, his ankles and his chest. The security guard moved away and for a minute Tad wriggled like a fish on dry land. But it was hopeless. He couldn't break free. He sank back and twisted his head—just in time to see another boy in what looked like a telephone booth disappear in an explosion of mauve steam. Tad shut his eyes. It was horrible! It was impossible!

And what were they going to do to *him*?

It was only now as he lay still that he became aware of the smell in the air. Strong air-conditioning had managed to get rid of most of it, but now, lying in the middle of the chamber, he felt almost suffocated by the smell of crushed strawberries. The strange thing was, the smell meant something to him. It reminded him of something. But what?

There was a movement in the corner of his eye and Tad turned back as the twin doctors approached, one holding a page of notes, the other a plastic bottle.

"What are you—" Tad began but stopped as his ear was given a sharp twist. Obviously the two men weren't in the mood to discuss things with him. Instead they muttered to each other.

"What's the active ingredient?"

"Very rare. Some sort of berry grown by the Arambayan Indians in Brazil. Just came in. The code is B/341."

Arambayan Indians. That meant something to Tad too. But, confused and frightened as he was, he couldn't remember where he had heard the words before.

One of the doctors opened the bottle and Tad recoiled, his skin crawling. One of the doctors called out and Marion Thorn approached, now wearing a white coat over her suit.

"Are you nervous, Bob?" she asked.

"Let me go!" Tad cried.

"There's nothing to worry about! We just want to rub something into your face. It's a special sort of cream. It's perfectly safe."

"Then why do you want to test it on me?"

Marion smiled again. "We know it's safe," she repeated. "And we know it's good for you. What we don't know, though, is *how* good it is for you. So that's why we want you to try it for us."

"Well, I don't want to." Tad pressed against the straps. "I want to go home!"

"You don't have a home, Bob," Marion replied reasonably. "That's why we brought you here." She leaned down and brushed the hair out of his eyes. "Let's not forget that you're a crook, Bob. A housebreaker. It's either here or the police."

"I choose the police!"

"I'm sorry, Bob. It's too late now."

Marion nodded and one of the twins squeezed a bright yellow cream into his gloved hand. The cream looked a little like custard, only thicker, and even at this distance it had a heavy, exotic smell. Positioning himself above Tad's head, the man rubbed some of the cream into Tad's face and neck, being careful to avoid his eyes, while the second man made notes. Soon Tad's face was completely coated. Marion Thorn walked away.

The cream was cool, not cold, and smelled of . . . it wasn't quite lemon and it wasn't quite pineapple but something in between. Despite himself, Tad had to admit that it was a very pleasant smell and he didn't even mind when the first man opened his dungarees and attached a wire to his chest. The cream was smooth and the smell was delicious. He could feel it invading his nostrils and seeping into his brain. *Pineapples and lemons say the bells of St. Clement's . . .* Next to him a machine began to bleep softly, in time with his heart.

"Slight dilation of the eyes," one of the twins muttered in a low voice. "How's his pulse?"

"Fast."

"This is nice," Tad said, slurring the words. "This is very, very nice."

"Loosen the straps," one of the men said. Or perhaps it was both of them. Tad's vision was beginning to blur.

"There's too much active ingredient."

"Moon fruit?"

"Yes."

"Let's leave him and see . . ."

"Moon. Goon. Balloon. See you soon," Tad replied, and giggled. Now that the straps had been loosened, he could move his hands and he tried to wipe some of the cream off. But his arms wouldn't obey him.

After that, everything seemed to stretch out of shape. Tad was hardly aware of the chamber anymore. He was floating, spinning, rocking, his mind far away. He thought the twins came back a couple of times. Once they wiped some of the cream off and added some cold liquid from a bottle. Another time they took his temperature. But he didn't care. He was above it all.

Somewhere an alarm went off and the boy who had been

doused in the mauve steam was carried away, his skin a mass of bright spots. A girl was led into the telephone booth in his place. Tad whimpered. The cream was less cool now. He could feel it burning his skin. But he was too weak and giddy to cry out. He twisted around on his bed, looking for Marion Thorn.

And then he saw a door open and a man step out. The man was far away, high up on a gantry, and Tad wasn't sure at first if he was imagining things. It had to be the cream that was doing it to him. It couldn't be true.

But then Marion Thorn approached the man. The two of them exchanged a few words and Marion laughed. The man took out a cigar and lit it. And suddenly Tad knew.

He was looking at the man behind ACID, the man who had set up the Center and who ran it.

Sir Hubert Spencer.

He was looking at his father.

BREAKOUT

It was as if Tad had been plunged into freezing water. The strange, dreamlike state that the cream had thrown him into was suddenly shattered and he was wide-awake, struggling with his thoughts, trying to make sense out of what he knew to be true.

The products in the Center. He knew what they all were, and had known from the moment he had been brought in.

The boy under the lamps was coated in grapefruit-and-aloe suntan oil. The girl with her feet in the bucket was testing coconut corn remover. The girl in the green foam was trying out a cucumber-and-kiwifruit bubble bath. The boy in the shower was being sprayed with body lotion made from different types of seaweed, while the one in the telephone booth was being subjected to a beetroot-and-banana body rub.

They were all products sold by Beautiful World. He had been seeing and smelling products like them all his life.

Beautiful World.

NONE OF OUR PRODUCTS ARE TESTED ON ANIMALS

But they were tested. *On children!*

Tad was horrified. A sudden bleeping made him turn his head and he saw that the machine he was connected to had speeded up. It was a heart monitor—of course! He watched, fascinated, as his heart, beating rapidly now, sent huge peaks across the screen. But at the same time he forced himself to calm down. The doctors had loosened his straps, believing him to be in a trance. If any of them looked at the machine, they would know otherwise and he would be strapped down again.

Tad lay back and closed his eyes. Gradually the heart monitor slowed and quieted. Could it be true? Beautiful World, owned by his parents, was taking kids off the street and using them as laboratory rats to test the safety of their products! And the charity that actually went out and found them—ACID— had also been set up by Sir Hubert and Lady Geranium.

But that was impossible. That would make them . . .

Monsters.

Tad took a deep breath, then opened his eyes again.

Bleep. Bleep. Bleep.

The heart monitor had almost exploded and there was nothing he could do to stop it. Sir Hubert Spencer had climbed down a metal staircase and was heading straight for him, Marion Thorn at his side. Now it took every ounce of Tad's willpower to bring himself back under control. He had to pretend to be drugged. It was his only chance.

"He's just over here, Sir Hubert..." Marion's voice reached his ears. Not trusting himself, Tad closed his eyes once again. Suddenly he felt the presence of the man standing right next to him.

His father.

His enemy.

No...!

"So this is the boy?" A wisp of cigar smoke crossed Tad's nostrils. "A nasty-looking piece of work. What's he testing?"

"The moon fruit, Sir Hubert. B/341."

"Any adverse effects?"

"It's much too strong, Sir Hubert. As you can see, the subject is virtually unconscious. There's also a little burning around the ears. Do you see?"

Tad felt Marion's finger drawing a line down the side of his face. How he managed to stop his heart from giving him away he would never know. As she withdrew the finger, the bleeping quickened again and he groaned, pretending to be having a bad dream.

"The little viper broke into my house, you know," Sir Hubert snarled. It was his own father, talking about him! But it was as if Tad were hearing his voice for the first time. "I don't want to see him again. Do you understand me?"

"Absolutely, Sir Hubert. We'll be testing that new microwave sauna for the first time tomorrow morning. I'd have said that Master Snarby was perfect for it. What do you think?"

Sir Hubert laughed. "Let me know what happens," he said.

The two of them walked away. Left to himself, Tad let out a great sigh and listened as the heart monitor once again resumed a steady pace. Even as Sir Hubert had been speaking, he had resisted the temptation to cry out, to try to explain who he really was. It would have been no good. He was sure of it. Sir Hubert wouldn't have listened, and it would have destroyed the one chance he had to get out of there.

The straps were loose. He was wide-awake. And nobody knew it.

Cautiously, Tad looked around. Sir Hubert and Marion Thorn were already some distance away and there was no sign of the twins. It must have been getting toward the end of the night, as the chamber was emptying. There were certainly fewer staff than when he had arrived.

Tad knew what he had to do. The very mention of a microwave sauna had been enough to conjure up the most horrible images. He had to get out of there before he ended up like a TV dinner and he had perhaps only seconds in which to do it.

Marion Thorn would be coming back to check on him. So would the twins. It had to be now!

Tad slipped one arm out of the straps and quickly unfastened the buckles on his chest and neck. Finally he bent double and freed his ankles. So far so good. Nobody had seen him. There was a cloth nearby and he used it to wipe off the moon-fruit cream. Marion had certainly been right about one thing. The skin on his cheeks was puffed up and sore. The cloth felt as if it were made of steel wool. Now, how did he get out of here? There was a door at the far end of the chamber— Sir Hubert and Marion had just passed through it, but the thought of running into the two of them was too horrible to contemplate. Then there were the elevators. But Tad remembered that they had no controls. He wouldn't even know how to call them and anyway they were too far away. That just left the metal staircase that Sir Hubert had taken. It had to be the right way. The chamber was underground. Tad had to go up.

Tad checked again that no one was looking, then pulled the heart monitor off his chest. That was his only mistake.

The connections were no sooner free than the machine began to scream, sending an alarm signal that could be heard from one side of the chamber to the other. Everybody turned. The twins appeared from behind a screen and began to move toward him. At the far end of the chamber a group of security guards ran forward, looking around to see where the disturbance had come from.

Tad swung himself onto his feet and took off. The first of

the twins reached him and grabbed hold of his arm. Tad twisted out of his grip and pushed as hard as he could. The twin was sent flying into a shelf of bottles that collapsed all around him, glass smashing and liquid splashing out. The twin screamed. One of the bottles must have contained acid. As Tad watched, the man's shoes began to dissolve.

Some of the other children were sitting up now, shouting encouragement. But the second twin had figured out where Tad was heading. The man, twice Tad's size, had positioned himself at the bottom of the stairs.

"All right," he began. "Don't move!"

There was a trolley loaded with bottles and test tubes, and as the second twin edged toward him, Tad grabbed it and propelled it forward. The trolley slammed into the man, glass falling and shattering all around. The twin was caught unprepared. The side of the trolley thumped into his stomach and at the same time his foot slipped. With a great shout he lost his balance and fell, crashing down onto his back. Tad leaped over him and onto the first step.

The other children were cheering him on, their cries echoing around the chamber. But the fastest of the security men had already reached the stairs, just behind Tad. Halfway up, Tad suddenly wheeled around and kicked out. His foot caught the man on the chin, knocking him over the banister and onto a work surface below. The security guard fell with a great cry, smashing into a row of test tubes and a Bunsen burner. The burner was still on. The jetting flame came into contact with the spilled chemicals and there was a satisfying *whumph* as a sheet of flame mushroomed to the ceiling. Immediately a bell began to ring. The sprinkler system switched on and suddenly Tad found himself climbing through a tropical storm. He was grateful for the water. It would add to the chaos. And it would wash the last of the cream from his face.

Tad reached the top of the stairs. There was a short corridor, then a door. He scrabbled for the handle, almost crying out with relief when it turned. Not daring to look back at the chaos he had left behind him, he jerked the door open and ran through, colliding with some sort of secretary who was just coming in. He didn't apologize. The woman fell in a shower of graphs and typewritten sheets. Tad leaped over her and ran down a wide, softly lit hallway.

He hadn't found a way out yet. This was some sort of storage area. One side of the hallway was lined with a series of large copper vats, each labeled FACE CREAM, FOOT LOTION, AFTER-SHAVE and so on. A pipe ran out of each of them, running up the wall to join a complicated network across the ceiling. The other side of the corridor contained a row of levers. Tad walked slowly past them. In front of him there was a double door. There was still nobody behind them.

He had almost reached the doors when they swung open and he found himself face-to-face with Marion Thorn.

She must have taken a second elevator, leaving Sir Hubert somewhere on the surface. Then, when the alarm was raised, she must have doubled back. But Tad didn't stop to consider how she had gotten there. He stared at the woman who had met him when he had been taken to ACID, hardly able to recognize her. Then he had thought her beautiful and kind. Now her eyes were bulging, her mouth was twisted in a grimace of hatred and her hair seemed to stand on end.

"You stay there!" she cried in a high-pitched voice, and to his amazement, Tad saw that she had produced a gun and was pointing it at him. She steadied it with both hands. "If you move, I'll shoot you in the heart."

Tad looked left and right. Behind him he could hear the commotion in the main chamber, the jangle of the alarm bells, the hiss of the sprinkler system. He wondered how long it would be before the security guards burst through the door. He knew he wouldn't get a second chance. If they caught him, he had a one-way ticket to the microwave. His eyes darted left and right. In a split second he had taken in the pipes, the levers, the position of the vats.

"I'm going to enjoy experimenting on you," the charity worker continued. She was confident now, enjoying her victory. "Sir Hubert warned me you were a nasty piece of work."

Tad looked down. "Please . . ." he muttered.

Marion Thorn threw back her head and laughed. It was what Tad had been waiting for.

He lunged to one side even as Marion lifted the gun and fired. The bullet missed him, passing over his head and ricocheting off a metal pipe. At the same moment, his hands found two of the levers. He pulled them. Marion aimed the gun again. But she was too late. The next moment there was a rush and a gurgle as two hundred gallons of bright red vanishing cream shot out of a pipe and crashed down onto the unfortunate woman.

Marion Thorn vanished.

Tad looked back. The door burst open and two more security guards appeared, both of them armed. Grateful now for the speed and agility he must have inherited from Bob Snarby, Tad twisted around and ran. There was an explosion and a bullet whistled past, smashing into a pipe close to Tad's head. A thin spray of pink ooze jetted into the air. Tad ran forward, vanishing cream licking at his ankles, and threw himself through the door.

And he was out! The cold night air embraced him and he ran into it with a sense of exhilaration. Quickly he took in the low redbrick buildings that made up the compound and the tall wire fence that surrounded it. Already an alarm had begun to let out its unnatural wail, and at the same time brilliant spotlights suddenly sliced through the darkness, huge white circles gliding across the asphalt.

Tad ran on, but with every step he found himself slowing down, realizing the hopelessness of his situation. There was no way out of the Center. The gate was too heavily guarded. The fence was unclimbable. And everywhere he looked there were more security guards, some on foot, some on motorbikes, making sure every square inch of the compound was covered.

"Security alert! Security alert!" The inhuman voice rang out across the rooftops. Tad stumbled and came to a breathless halt.

On the other side of the fence he could see houses. In the distance there was a pub. He almost wanted to cry. The real world, ordinary people doing ordinary things, were only a few yards away. But he couldn't reach them. He would never see them again. There was no way out.

"There he is!"

It was a man's voice, coming from just behind him. To one side a Jeep suddenly sprang forward, its headlights slanting down. Tad stood where he was. There was nothing more he could do.

And then it happened. At the last minute, just when he thought it was all over, there was the blare of a horn and a London taxi appeared out of nowhere, accelerating toward the fence. Tad watched as it burst through, snapping the wire, and hurtled toward him. Meanwhile the Jeep had also accelerated and suddenly the two vehicles were heading straight for each other in what had to be a head-on collision. It was the driver of the Jeep who lost his nerve. With mere inches to spare, he wrenched the wheel. The Jeep swerved, crashed into a building and disappeared in a pillar of flame. The taxi screeched to a halt in front of Tad and the back door opened.

"Get in!" a voice commanded.

Tad hesitated. But then there was a gunshot and a bullet hammered into the taxi's chassis, and without any further prompting, Tad dived forward. His head and arms passed through the open door and he was full length on the back floor and the voice was yelling, "Go! Go! Go!" The taxi leaped forward again, made a complete circle and shot through the hole in the fence. There were more shots. The back window shattered and fell inward, covering Tad with glass. The driver cursed as the taxi mounted the pavement then rocketed into the road. But they were away! Around one corner and through a set of red traffic lights and they had left the Center far behind.

Tad lay where he was, stretched out on the floor. He was bruised and exhausted and there was glass in his hair and all over his clothes. But he was safe.

"All right. You can sit up now."

Tad recognized the voice and felt the hairs on his neck prickle. A hand reached down and dragged him into the seat. Tad slumped back, the last of his strength draining out of him.

"Good evening, Bobby-boy," Finn said. "What a surprise—eh! We been looking all over for you."

GREAT YARMOUTH

Aren't you pleased to see me?" Finn demanded.

"And me!" The driver peered over his shoulder and grinned. It was Eric Snarby. He had a broken cigarette between his lips. In all the excitement he'd bitten it in half.

"Keep your eye on the road, Snarby," Finn snapped. "And your foot on the axe-hellerator. We got a long way to go!"

Tad turned to Finn. "How did you find me?" he asked.

Finn brushed broken glass off his shoulders. The whole of the window had fallen in, but fortunately it was a warm night—and a dry one. "I been looking for you ever since that little business in Nightingale Square," he explained. "In fact I 'ad the 'ole network out. All over London. The street vendors and the traffic cops. The thieves and the beggars. The cleaners, the cabbies and the couriers. I was worried about you, you see, my boy. I was worried about what might 'appen to you."

"You mean, you were worried I'd be picked up by the police."

"I wanted to find you." They drove past a streetlamp and for a moment the skin behind the spiderweb glowed a horrible orange. "And you're lucky I did, Bobby-boy. If old Finn hadn't come looking for you, 'oo knows what would 'ave 'appened to you. Shampooed to death, perhaps. Or bubblebathed till you was insane . . ."

Tad leaned forward. "You know about the Center!" he exclaimed.

Finn smiled. "There's nothing happens in London that Finn don't know about," he replied. "And the nastier it is, the sooner I hear . . ."

Tad twisted in his seat and looked out of the broken window. The street behind them was empty. "Where are we going?" he asked.

"You might as well lie back and catch a few z's," Finn replied. "We're going to the country. Life in town's a bit 'ot for old Finn at the moment. We're going to join the carnival."

"Great Yarmouth!" Tad remembered the Snarbys talking about the move.

"That's right. Boring, snoring, rain-always-pouring Great Yarmouth. But we can lie low there and work out how to earn a dishonest penny or two."

"Your mum'll be glad to see you!" Eric crooned from the front seat.

"Shut up and keep your eye on the road!" Finn snapped.

"And get a move on, for Gawd's sake. You're only doing a hundred miles an hour!"

Eric Snarby slammed his foot on the pedal and the taxi leaped forward, racing into the night.

The boardwalk at Great Yarmouth was a true, permanent, old-fashioned amusement park. It was more wood than plastic, more falling apart than thrilling. All in all there were about thirty rides, dominated by a huge roller coaster that stretched out parallel with the sea. There were bumper cars, of course, a leaky water flume, a cyclone and a ghost train so old that it could have been haunted by the ghosts of people who had once ridden it. Its most recent attraction was a Mirror Maze, a circular building mounted with speakers so that anyone passing could hear the cries and laughter of the people inside. But the Mirror Maze, like the rest of the park, was closed. It was seven-thirty in the morning. And, as Tad gazed up at the highest loop of the roller coaster, he was utterly alone.

Eric Snarby had a caravan just across the road from the boardwalk and he and Finn had gone in to get a few hours' sleep. Doll had not yet woken up. There wouldn't have been enough room for Tad, even if he had been tired. But he'd slept in the taxi. He was glad to be on his own.

He needed to think.

It was still so hard to believe. His parents, Sir Hubert and Lady Geranium Spencer, running a business that used children in experiments? The brains behind a charity that horribly exploited the young people who needed its help? It was impossible, unthinkable. His parents were decent people. His father had been knighted by the queen! But as hard as he tried to persuade himself that his parents were somehow innocent, that they knew nothing, Tad couldn't make it work.

In the distance, the waves rolled and broke against the beach hidden behind the roller coaster. The sun had risen, but the sky was still gray. Tad shivered and walked on.

What made it so difficult was that he wasn't even sure anymore who he was. Was he Tad Spencer or was he Bob Snarby? He looked like Bob. He was beginning to talk like him and to think like him. And (it was only now that he realized it) he was even beginning to enjoy some aspects of being Bob. It was crazy, but that was the truth. He liked being thin. He liked being fit, able to run without wheezing and to climb without trembling. It was true that he had lost all his wealth, his toys, his comfortable house and servants, but in a strange way he felt almost relieved, as if it were a weight off his shoulders.

There wasn't a lot to admire about Bob Snarby or his background, but at least he was free. Tad wasn't sure if he was Tad or if he was Bob, but for the first time in his life he felt he was himself.

But what was he going to do?

He couldn't stay with Eric and Doll Snarby, not if that meant working for Finn. At the same time he had nowhere else to go. And then there was the real Bob Snarby to consider. Tad remembered his meeting with the fat boy in Knightsbridge. Could he allow Bob Snarby to remain in his place? It didn't seem fair. It didn't seem right.

He looked up and blinked. Although he hadn't noticed it before, there was one caravan in the park, an old-fashioned Gypsy-style caravan, that he would have recognized even without the sign above the door:

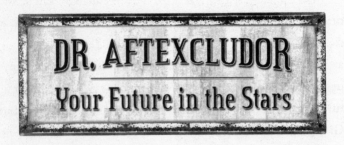

DR. AFTEXCLUDOR
Your Future in the Stars

Tad stared at it. The caravan was parked next to the ghost train, and even at this early hour the door was open. Tad thought back to his last meeting with the caravan's peculiar owner. Dr. Aftexcludor had known who he was. He had seemed—at least in part—sympathetic. And he had told some crazy story about wishing stars . . . how they had caused the switch. False name, false story, Tad thought now. Perhaps this was the right time to find out the truth.

Tad went over to the caravan and looked inside. There was no sign of the doctor or his curious Indian friend, Solo. Tad climbed in.

The thick smell of incense filled his nostrils and he was once again amazed by how the caravan seemed so much bigger inside than out.

"Dr. Aftexcludor . . . ?" he called softly.

There was a book, lying open on the table, next to the

crystal ball. Tad almost got the feeling that it had been left there for him to find. Moving forward, he turned a page. The paper was old and heavy and really not like paper at all. Tad looked down and began to read.

Two pages were exposed and there was a naked figure drawn on each one, two boys connected by a complicated series of arrows. The figures were surrounded by stars, planets and other astrological devices and some of the arrows pointed up toward these. The book was handwritten, the sentences tumbling into one another and slanting in different directions. Growing ever more uneasy, Tad realized what the book reminded him of. It was like something out of a fairy story. A book of spells.

There were two words written in red, but the ink was so old that it had lost most of its color. Tad ran a finger across them. "The Switch." Underneath, a line of writing twisted in a curve. "Janus. The star of change. Invoking its power. To effect the switch between two personalities . . ." Tad didn't understand all of it, but he understood enough. Anger exploded inside him along with shock and disbelief. He picked up the ancient book and was about to throw it across the room when . . .

"Master Snarby! How nice to see you again."

Tad whirled around. He hadn't heard anyone come in, but now Dr. Aftexcludor was standing right behind him, dressed in a dark green velvet jacket and baggy pantaloons. The Indian, Solo, was with him, standing in the doorway, blocking it.

"I'm not Bob Snarby!" Tad snarled. "I'm Tad Spencer. You know that. You're the one who did it!"

"Did what?" Dr. Aftexcludor looked the picture of innocence.

"You know!" Tad pointed at the open book. "All that stuff you told me about 'wishing stars' was nonsense and you know it! You're responsible. You're some sort of—"

Magician? Tad stopped himself before he actually uttered the word. It was ridiculous. Real magicians didn't exist, did they? Not real ones. But after what had happened to him, he suddenly realized, anything was possible.

"You did it," he repeated weakly.

"Why should I have wanted to?" Dr. Aftexcludor asked reasonably.

"I don't know. But . . ." Tad remembered now. "There was something you were going to tell me. Something about Solo."

"Ah yes." Dr. Aftexcludor moved forward and sat down, cross-legged, at the table. He might have looked old, but his movements were still somehow those of a younger man. "I was going to tell you a story," he said.

"You said I wasn't ready."

"Are you now, Tad? Do you want to hear it?"

"Yes."

Dr. Aftexcludor nodded. "Yes. I think so. Draw closer, Tad, Bob, whatever you want to call yourself."

Tad sat opposite the old man. There was a crystal ball on

the table and he found himself fixated by it, by the colors that seemed to swirl around inside it. Dr. Aftexcludor muttered something in the strange language that he had used before and Solo retired. Tad glanced at him as he disappeared into the next room.

"You said Solo was an Arambayan Indian," Tad said.

"Yes. The last of the tribe."

Arambayan Indians. Moon fruit. Suddenly Tad knew what this was all about.

His eyes were fixed on the crystal ball and he couldn't have broken away if he had tried to. And now it was as if shapes were forming themselves out of the colors. Maybe it was him. Maybe it was all the smoke in the room that was somehow sending him to sleep, but it was as if he were looking through the reflection on a pool and into the world beneath. It was a forest. He had never seen so much green, believed there could be so many different shades. There were flowers, brilliant colors. He could smell them! And now he could hear the rushing of a great river as the images rose and drew him into them.

And all the time he heard the voice of Dr. Aftexcludor, coming as if from miles away, telling him the terrible story that he was seeing with his own eyes.

"The Amazon basin," he began. "The rain forest west of Manaus. Denser and wilder than anywhere in the world. There are not many places where man has not at some time trodden on this wretched planet, Tad, but not in the rain forests. The rain forests are the last great uncharted territory . . .

even if the bulldozers are doing their work and the lands are rapidly dwindling.

"There was a tribe of Indians here called the Arambayans. They were not even discovered by white men until 1947, Tad, just after the war. Westerners found them and for a time did them no harm. They were visited by missionaries. And they began to trade—for there was a fruit that grew in the Arambayans' land . . . a fruit that looked like a crescent moon and tasted of pineapples and lemon."

"The moon fruit!" Tad exclaimed, and saw it, hanging in clusters, brilliant yellow moons against a swath of dark green leaves.

"The moon fruit," Dr. Aftexcludor repeated. "Now, all would have been well except that the fame of this new and delicious fruit spread across the globe. And a man heard about it. He tasted it. And he decided that he wanted to buy it. All of it."

"Who was this man?" Tad whispered.

"I'll come to that. The trouble is, the Arambayans were a very suspicious people. You see, they'd always been very happy just the way they were. They were peaceful. They just got on with their lives, raising their families and growing their fruit. They sold enough to meet their immediate needs. But their needs, you see, were small.

"They didn't trust this man-from-over-the-seas, and they didn't want anything to do with him. The more money he offered them, the less they trusted him. So when he offered to buy all their moon fruit, they politely but firmly said no.

"Unfortunately the man wouldn't take no for an answer. He still wanted the moon fruit. And so he did a terrible thing . . ."

The crystal ball had gone dark now. It was showing Tad a tropical night sky. But now he saw lights gliding through the darkness. A helicopter. It landed on a rough strip hacked out of the jungle. Tad knew that he was watching something secretive, something wrong. The blades of the helicopter began to slow down and the pilot stepped out. Tad recognized him. It was his father's chauffeur: Spurling.

"I said that the Arambayans didn't like war," Dr. Aftexcludor continued, "but they did have enemies. There was a tribe on the edge of the territory who had always been jealous of them and it was to this tribe, the Cruel People, that the man-from-over-the-seas turned. Suppose they were to own the moon fruit, would they sell it to him? And at a reasonable price? A deal was struck. And one dark night the Cruel People were given what they needed to take what wasn't theirs."

Spurling had heaved three wooden crates out of the helicopter. He was surrounded by black, painted faces now, their expressions ugly and menacing.

"He supplied them with guns. Oh—it's been done before, Tad! The Arambayans had blowpipes, bows and arrows, spears. But now their enemy, the Cruel People, had joined the twentieth century. They had guns. Automatic rifles. And fueled by alcohol and greed, they attacked their poor neighbors."

Dr. Aftexcludor fell silent, but the crystal ball told its own story. He saw the Arambayan village, a circle of straw-covered huts on the edge of a river. He saw the women with their children, the men swimming and laughing in the clear water. Then there was a shot. It came from the edge of the forest. A young boy, barely older than Tad, was thrown wounded to the ground and then the Cruel People were on them, swarming over the village as more shots rang out and the flames rose from the first of the houses.

Tad covered his eyes. He couldn't take any more.

"It was my father," he muttered. "It was Sir Hubert Spencer and Beautiful World."

"Solo was one of the very few who escaped alive," Dr. Aftexcludor went on. "You might say he's the last of the Arambayans. I've looked after him ever since, but he has no real life . . ." His voice trailed away. "I'm sorry," he said at length. "But you said you wanted to hear. You said you were ready."

"I know." Tad felt an intense sadness, deeper than anything he had experienced in his life. It was as if a river were running through him. "I had to know," he said at last. "And . . . I suppose . . . I'm glad I know now."

"Yes."

Tad stood up. Suddenly he knew what he had to do. "Good-bye, Dr. Aftexcludor," he said. "Thank you."

"Good-bye, Tad. And good luck."

Tad paused at the door. "There is one thing," he said. "Will I . . . will you ever change me back into Tad Spencer?"

Dr. Aftexcludor shook his head. "Only you can do that," he said. "You can be what—and who—you want to be."

Tad left. He never saw Dr. Aftexcludor again.

. . .

When Tad got back to the caravan, Eric and Doll Snarby had finally woken up and were once again tucking into a mountainous breakfast, this time consisting entirely of kippers. Tad had never seen so many kippers slipping and slithering over one another on one plate. Finn was sitting in a corner, smoking a cigarette.

"My Bob!" Doll sobbed by way of greeting. "Back 'ome at last!" She picked up one of the kippers and used it to wipe her nose. "I been so worried about you!"

"It's true," Eric added. "Your mum's been worrying 'erself to death. Some nights she's only managed nine pizzas."

"My little boy!" Doll sniffed.

"And a dozen Mars bars. She 'ad a dozen Mars bars. But apart from that, she couldn't eat a thing!"

"Shut up, the two of you," Finn snapped, and the Snarbys fell silent. Finn leaned forward and held something up, a narrow book with a blue cover. His eyes locked into Tad's. "Where did you get this, you thieving vermin?" he demanded.

Tad recognized the checkbook that he had taken from his own bedroom in Knightsbridge. His hand fell automatically to his back pants pocket.

"It was in the back of the cab," Finn explained. "Must 'ave slipped out your back pocket."

"It's mine!" Tad said.

"Yours, is it? That's funny. 'Cause it 'asn't got your name in it." Finn opened the checkbook. "'Thomas Arnold David Spencer,'" he read. He scratched his cheek, his nails rasping against three days' stubble. "So who's he?" he demanded.

"Leave the boy alone, Finn," Doll said.

"You stay out of this, Doll, or by heaven, I'll pull your leg off and kick you with it." Finn turned back to Tad. "Who is he?"

"He's no one. Some rich kid. He's the son of Sir Hubert Spencer. You know . . ."

"Sir Hubert Spencer, Beautiful World?" Finn weighed the checkbook in his hand. "Pickpocketed it, did you?"

"Yes."

"What did I tell you about stealing!" Eric Snarby leaned forward and slapped Tad hard on the side of his head. "If you're going to steal something, make sure you can sell it. A checkbook's no blooming good! Why didn't you get 'is watch?"

"Wait a minute. Wait a minute . . ." Finn was thinking. You could almost see the thoughts passing one at a time across his eyes. "The Spencers, they got a place down near Ipswich," he muttered. "Snatchmore Hall or something . . ."

"What—you going to burgle it?" Doll asked.

"Not burgle it. No." Finn raised the checkbook to his nostrils and sniffed it. He let out a pleasurable sigh. "A rich kid with his own bank account, that's given old Finn a thought. Maybe burgling ain't the right game for us. Maybe there's an easier way . . ."

"What you got in mind, Finn?" Eric demanded.

"You wait and see," Finn replied. "Just you wait and see."

PRIME STEAK

Tad clung to the branch of the oak tree, his dangling feet only inches from the razor wire and broken glass below. Using all his strength, he swung one hand in front of the other and passed over the garden wall. If he dropped onto the ground now, he would break both his legs, but just as he remembered there would be, a great pile of grass clippings had been left, close to the wall. Tad gritted his teeth, then let go with both hands. He fell, hit the pile and sank to his waist in the cut grass. Fortunately, the weather had been dry. The grass was old and soggy, but not the mush he had feared.

He stood up inside the grounds of Snatchmore Hall, the home that had once been his.

He made his way quickly toward the house, taking care not to be seen. As he drew closer, he ducked behind trees or ran crouching from bush to bush. At last he came to the edge of the lawn with the swimming pool to one side and the side entrance to the house just ahead. As he paused, catching his breath, there was a sudden movement and he ducked back out of sight. A car had started up and was rolling down the driveway toward the main gate. Tad caught sight of Spurling behind the wheel. And where was the grim-faced chauffeur off to now? he wondered. Looking for more children to invite to the Center? Or perhaps selling more weapons to wipe out another uncooperative Indian tribe?

The car passed through the electronic gates, which swung smoothly shut behind it. At least that was one less danger to have to worry about. He had already seen Mrs. O'Blimey leave the house to go shopping. Mitzy was on vacation. Lady Geranium Spencer would still be in bed.

That just left Bob Snarby. On his own.

Tad had to cross about a hundred yards of open ground to reach the safety of the house and he was once again grateful for this new body of his. He could cover the ground in less than a minute. He tensed himself, then darted forward.

And stopped.

Finn and he had planned all this carefully, taking into account the electronic gates, the wall, the video cameras and the trip wires concealed in the garden. But they had forgotten the last security measure in the house—and now it was too late.

Vicious had sprung out as if from nowhere. The oversize dalmatian stood in front of him, its hackles rising, its lips pulled back to reveal its specially sharpened teeth. There was a savage hunger in its eyes as it padded forward, its paws barely seeming to touch the ground. Tad remembered the last intruder to come across Vicious, the 107 stitches the man had needed. When he had left the hospital, he had looked like a jigsaw puzzle.

Tad looked around. He was right out in the open, with nowhere to run. If he turned and tried to make it back to the trees, the dog would be on him before he had taken three paces. It was about to spring. Every single part of the creature was poised for the attack. Tad closed his eyes and prepared for the worst.

"You can be what—and who—you want to be."

It was as if the words had been whispered in his ear. They were virtually the last words that Dr. Aftexcludor had spoken to him, and remembering them now, Tad suddenly had an idea.

He opened his eyes and held out his hand, palm down, showing it to the dog.

"Vicious . . ." he muttered.

The dog growled again.

"Good old Vicious! Don't you know me, boy? It's Tad! You remember me!"

The dog looked at him blankly. And it didn't stop growling.

"You know it's me!" Tad insisted. He tapped his chest. "I'm in here. I know it's not my body, but it's still me. You're not going to hurt me, are you!"

And then the dalmatian wagged its tail! It recognized him!

Tad let out his breath in a huge sigh of relief. Vicious was drooling now, expecting an éclair. Tad pointed with one finger. "Basket!" he commanded.

"Basket!" Tad said again.

The dog turned and ran into the house. Tad watched it go with a sense of elation. It wasn't just that he had survived the encounter. It was something more. Despite his new face, his new clothes, even his new smell, he now realized that deep down there *was* still a part of him that was Tad Spencer. And always would be.

With more hope and excitement than he had felt in weeks, Tad ran the rest of the way and went in through the kitchen door.

He had known it would be open. Mrs. O'Blimey was always forgetting to lock it, and as Tad had suspected, the kitchen was empty. There was a second door on the other side and he went through it, passing into a small, bare room filled with television monitors, video recorders and other equipment; the security room of Snatchmore Hall.

Tad sat down in front of a console. Set in the panel opposite him was a color television screen showing a wobbling image of the main gates. Next to it was a grid with ten numbered buttons and a microphone. Tad punched in a code: 1–10–8.

There was a buzz and the gates swung open.

Tad kept his eyes on the screen. A battered white van had appeared with IPSWICH SLAUGHTERHOUSE—LOVELY FRESH MEAT painted on the side. Finn had stolen the van the day before and it was, of course, he who was behind the wheel. As he drove through the gates and onto the driveway, he leaned out of the window and gave a thumbs-up sign to the closed-circuit camera. Tad pressed the buttons again and the gates closed.

He was waiting for Finn by the kitchen door when the van arrived. Finn killed the engine and got out. "Any trouble?" he demanded.

"No," Tad replied. "The chauffeur's out. There's no sign of the servants. And Mum . . . I mean . . . Lady Geranium must still be in bed."

"Good boy! Good boy!" Finn reached into the van and pulled out a sack. Perhaps it really had been used for carrying meat once, as it was old and stained and smelled horrible. "Right. Let's go," he said.

The two of them set off on tiptoe through the house. Everything felt unreal to Tad—just as it had when he'd broken into the mews house in London. To be in his home yet at the same time an intruder, breaking the law . . . it made him dizzy just to think about it. But he couldn't tell Finn that. In fact, it almost amused him, pretending that he was here for the first time.

"What a place! What a place!" Finn whispered as they crossed the main hall and made for the stairs. There was a little antique table leaning against a wall and Finn stopped beside it. He picked up a silver cigarette box and held it to the light. "Worth a few bucks," he whispered.

"That's not what we're here for," Tad reminded him in a low voice.

"Shame to leave it, though." Finn slipped the box into his

pocket and crept on. The two of them climbed the stairs and started along a corridor, Finn softly opening each door he came to and peering into the room behind. The door they wanted was the fifth on the right. Tad could have found his way to it blindfolded. But once again, he said nothing. He would let Finn do it his way.

A bathroom. A sauna. An empty bedroom. A dressing room. Finn reached the fifth door and opened it. The sound of snoring rose and fell in the half-light. Finn whistled softly and hitched up the sack. Tad followed him into what had once been his bedroom.

It was a wreck. The carpet was almost completely hidden by the candy wrappers, potato-chip bags, cookie boxes, crumpled comics, old socks and smelly underwear that covered it. The neat shelves of books and computer games (his books, his computer games!) had been torn apart and one of the computers had a broken screen and grape jelly all over the keyboard. One wall had been covered by a zigzagging line of spray paint. The whole room stank of cigarette smoke.

Finn took this all in and smiled. "He treats his room just like you do, Bob," he muttered.

"Shhh!" Tad's eyes had been drawn to the bed, where the room's occupant lay, his stomach in the air, snoring heavily. Once again Tad had the strange sensation of realizing that he was looking at himself, but this time he felt only disgust. The boy on the bed resembled nothing so much as a huge jellyfish. His arms and legs were splayed out and his silk pajamas had slipped down to reveal a great, swollen belly. Rolls of fat bulged underneath the pajamas, and as the boy breathed they moved—but in different directions. Bob Snarby had fallen asleep with his mouth wide open and there was a bead of saliva caught between his upper and lower lip that quivered each time he snored.

"Is this really me?" Tad muttered. "Was this me?"

"What?" Finn hissed.

"Nothing."

"What a slob!" Finn muttered. "I hope the sack's big enough!"

Tad and Finn crept forward, right up to the sleeping boy. They exchanged a glance. "Now!" Finn said.

Together they pounced. Bob Snarby didn't even have time to open his eyes before he found himself grabbed and half buried in the foul-smelling sack. As Finn hoisted him up, Tad pulled. The sack slid over Bob's head, down his body and over his feet. As the end came clear, Finn produced a length of rope and tied it in a tight knot. "Prime steak," he muttered, and grinned at his own joke. "Now let's get him loaded up."

A few minutes later the gates of Snatchmore Hall opened for a second time and the white butcher's van rocketed out and veered off down the lane. Finn was gripping the wheel, staring out with wide, manic eyes. Tad was sitting next to him. The sack was kicking and squirming in the back.

Lady Geranium Spencer woke up at noon exactly, nicely in time for either a late breakfast or an early lunch. She had a slight headache and was feeling depressed after what had been a depressing evening. She and Sir Hubert had taken dear Tad to a performance of Shakespeare's *Comedy of Errors.* Tad should have loved it. It was his favorite play, and as this was a touring production from Athens, it was actually in Greek. But instead of being pleased, Tad had been ghastly. He had complained through Act One, slept through Act Two, eaten too much ice cream during intermission and then thrown up in Act Three. Lady Geranium groaned quietly. The truth was, Tad hadn't been the same since he fell off that horse. Not the same at all.

She got up and went into the bathroom. She paused in front of the mirror and gave a little scream. A hideous brown face stared back at her. Then she remembered. She had gone to bed with a mud pack on her face, but she had been so tired she had forgotten to take it off.

Half an hour later, wrapped in a dressing gown, Lady Geranium walked down the corridor on her way to the breakfast room. She passed her son's bedroom and looked in. To her surprise there was no sign of the boy. The room was as horrible as ever . . . after twenty-five years of loyal service, Mrs. O'Blimey had submitted her resignation a few days before and Mitzy still wasn't back following her nervous breakdown.

"Tad?" Lady Geranium called out.

There was no answer, but then Lady Geranium noticed an envelope pinned to the door. It was addressed to SIR HUBERT AND LADY GERANIUM SPENCER. SNATCHMORE HALL. But the words hadn't been written. They had been torn out of newspapers and magazines.

Puzzled and slightly alarmed, she took the envelope down

and opened it. There was a single sheet of white paper inside and on it a message, also set down in letters that had been cut out and glued into place.

WE HAVe YOUR SON. dO NOt CALL tHE POLICE OR YOU WILL NEVeR SEE HIM AGAIN. BRING ONE MILLION dOLLARS IN A SUItCASe tO GREAt YARMOUtH PARk At MIDNIGHt tONIGHt. LEAVE It At tHe ENtRANCE tO tHE BIG DIPPER. NO tRICkS. NO POLICE. YOU HAVe BEeN WARNED.

Lady Geranium read the note three times. Then she ran to the telephone and called Sir Hubert.

DARK THOUGHTS

Sir Hubert Spencer held the ransom note in his shaking hands and read it for the twenty-seventh time. His face, never handsome at the best of times, was taut and twisted with anger.

"It's an outrage!" he exclaimed—and not for the first time either. "They won't get away with it!"

"Taking our boy!" Lady Geranium sobbed.

"I'm not talking about the boy!" Sir Hubert exploded. "It's me I'm thinking about! How dare they try to threaten *me*? Don't they know who I am?"

Sir Hubert paced up and down the room like a tiger in a cage. His wife watched him anxiously. "Can you come up with the money?" she asked. "A million dollars! It seems like an awful lot."

"Of course I can come up with the money," Sir Hubert snapped. "The question is, do I want to?"

Lady Geranium stared at him. "What do you mean?"

"Well, the fact is, my dear . . . I wonder if young Tad is actually worth it."

"What?"

"Ever since he fell off that damn horse, he hasn't been the same. He's stupid. He's slovenly at the table. He doesn't speak French, German or Greek anymore. He's messy. The truth of the matter is, I'm beginning to wonder if this kidnap business mightn't be a blessing in disguise."

Lady Geranium thought for a moment. "It is true," she said in a low voice. "He has changed. Do you think, if we don't pay . . . they might just keep him?"

Just then there was a knock at the door.

"Come in!" Sir Hubert called.

The door opened and the chauffeur, Spurling, came in, looking as dapper as ever in a freshly ironed uniform. But his eyes were dark and his face was grim. "Forgive me for interrupting you, sir," he began.

"Go on, Spurling . . ."

The chauffeur coughed discreetly, like a doctor about to give bad news. "I've been studying the film, sir. The film taken this afternoon by the security camera at the gate. I think there's something you ought to see . . ."

The three figures stood, huddled together in the empty fairgrounds, completely dwarfed by the great bulk of the roller coaster that towered behind them. Somewhere on the other side of it, lost in the darkness, the waves rolled in. They sounded slow and heavy. There was something wrong with the night. The air was too warm. There was no breeze at all. And the sky was tinted an unnatural shade of purple—as if it were in pain.

"There's going to be a storm," Eric Snarby said.

"It's a 'orrible night," his wife agreed.

"Shut up!" Finn hissed, and glanced at his two companions, who pursed their lips and looked away.

Finn was holding a radio transmitter and now he pressed a black button on the side. "Testing, testing. One, two, three . . ."

"I can hear you, Finn. Loud and clear." Tad's voice came back thin and disembodied. He could have been anywhere, but in fact he was on the other side of the road in the Snarbys' caravan.

"You all right, Bobby-boy?" Finn held the transmitter only inches from his lips. "'Ow's our guest?"

"Trussed up like a Christmas turkey and twice as fat," came the reply. "I'm fine, Finn."

"All right. Robert and out." Finn clicked the transmitter off and grinned. "You know what this is?" he said. "This is the perfect plan!"

"You said that the last time," Eric muttered.

"And the time before," Doll added.

"This time I got it all worked out. The Spencer kid is in the caravan with Bob—but nobody knows that. Only us. Now, at midnight, I'll be at the roller coaster. His lordship will come with the money. The two of you will be watching from the ghost train . . ."

"I don't like ghosts," Doll said.

"It's only plastic! It can't 'urt you!"

"Go on, Finn . . ." Eric rasped. He was looking pale and nervous. Perhaps it was just the heat of the night, but there was a film of sweat on his forehead and cheeks and his sty was wet and glistening. His whole head looked like a rotten fruit.

"You'll 'ave a radio transmitter," Finn went on. "When I got the money and I know everything's all right, I'll signal you. That's when I 'op it. You signal Bob and tell 'im to bring the Spencer boy over. Then you leave too."

"What if it's a trick?" Doll asked. "What if it's the police what turn up?"

Finn shook his head. "They won't risk the police," he said. "These rich types—they treat their kids like precious jewels. They wouldn't do nothing to hurt little Tad. No. I'll get the money and I'll be gone. You Snarbys'll 'ave plenty of time to get clear. And then we'll all meet in London and we'll be rich!"

"What about Bob?" Eric asked. "If 'e 'ands over the boy, they'll 'ave 'im!"

Finn smiled slowly, his silver fillings glinting in the night. "We don't need Bob anymore," he said. "He's not the same anymore. 'E 'asn't been the same since that business with the glue. 'E let me down badly in Nightingale Square and I been thinking . . . maybe it's time 'e spent a bit of time with 'Er Majesty."

"Prison?" Doll muttered.

"They'll only give 'im a few years. It'll do 'im good." Finn was friendly now, simpering at both the Snarbys. "You won't miss 'im," he added. "Another couple of years and 'e'd 'ave left 'ome anyway."

"That's true," Eric Snarby said.

Finn slid his walking stick through his belt and took the Snarbys' arms in his hands. "A million bucks!" he said. "And one less to share it with." He laughed quietly. "Now let's go and get a drink."

Tad put the transmitter down and drew back the curtain. Bob Snarby was lying on Eric and Doll's bed, his hands tied behind him, his ankles taped together and a gag drawn tight across his mouth. As soon as he saw Tad, he began to squirm, rocking his body back and forth and trying to shout out. But the gag cut off virtually any noise and all Bob could do was plead with the other boy with his eyes.

"I'll undo the gag," Tad said. "But if you shout out, I'll put it right on again. Do you understand?"

"Mmmmm!" Bob jerked his head up and down.

Tad went over to him and untied the gag. It was an old scarf of Doll's and he dreaded to think what it tasted like. As soon as the cloth fell free, Bob opened his mouth and drew in a great breath. Tad was tensed, ready to pounce on him—but Bob didn't shout. To Tad's astonishment, he simply burst into tears.

For the first time, Tad actually felt sorry for the other boy.

Lying there with tears streaming down his pudgy cheeks, his fancy clothes all wrinkled and disarrayed, he really looked pathetic. Bob Snarby probably hadn't cried since the day he was born. But it seemed that he had changed. It seemed that they both had.

"It's all right," Tad said. "No one's going to 'urt you."

"You already have hurt me!" the other boy replied. His voice was petulant. Tad had often used that voice when he couldn't get what he wanted.

"Do you want a cup of tea, Bob?" There was no reply.

"Would you prefer it if I called you Tad?"

"No . . ."

Tad gazed at his prisoner. "It seems to me that you *are* Tad now," he said. "And I *am* Bob. We really have switched!"

"Is that why you've done this?" the other boy cried. "You've kidnapped me because you're jealous that I've taken your place."

"No." Tad smiled. "You probably won't believe me, but I don't want to switch back anymore." Even Tad was surprised by what he had just said. It was as if he'd only just realized it himself. But now he saw the boy he had been—a great, spoiled ball of flab in an expensive suit. He remembered how his parents had earned the money that had turned him into that. And he knew that it was true. He could never go back. Not to Snatchmore Hall. Not to them. "I don't want to be Tad Spencer anymore," he said. "I think I'm happier being you."

Bob tugged at his cords again, but Finn had tied them and they stayed firm. "So why *have* you kidnapped me?" he asked.

"It was Finn who kidnapped you," Tad said. "He did it for the money and I didn't have any choice. But I've been doing a bit of thinking and I've got a plan of my own."

"What plan?"

"That's my business." Tad smiled. "But you listen to me, Tad Spencer. You do exactly what I say, when I say it. And everything's going to be all right."

In the security room at Snatchmore Hall, Sir Hubert Spencer sat down in front of the television screen.

The cameras had caught a figure running from the edge of the shrubbery across the lawn. Spurling had frozen the image and now he closed in on it until a boy's face filled the screen. The image was hazy, distorted at the edges but still recognizable.

"I know him!" Lady Geranium exclaimed.

"We all know him!" Sir Hubert snarled. "He's the little brat you found at the mews house. The one you sent over to ACID."

"The one who escaped from the Center!" Lady Geranium's face had gone white . . . all of it apart from her nose. After so many operations, the nose seemed to have a life of its own. Sometimes it even blew itself when she wasn't expecting it. "So what was he doing here?" she asked.

"A very good question, my dear."

"Do you think it was a coincidence?"

"No. I don't."

Sir Hubert stared at the image on the screen. With a shaking finger he drew a line across Tad's face. "First the mews. Then the Center. Now here." There was a long silence. "This boy—Bob Snarby—must know about us. Beautiful World. The experiments. Everything!"

Spurling coughed discreetly. "Would you like me to deal with him, sir?" he asked.

"Yes, Spurling. I would."

The chauffeur reached into his jacket and drew out a slim black revolver: a Davis P-380 .38 automatic.

"What are you going to do?" Lady Geranium asked.

"Don't worry yourself, my dear," Sir Hubert said. "This kidnapping may be just what we need. Great Yarmouth amusement park at midnight? That's where the boy will be . . . along with his accomplices."

"If you want me to murder them all, sir, might I suggest the TEC-9 automatic machine gun?" Spurling said.

"No, Spurling." Sir Hubert smiled. "Your job is to get the boy. Just the boy." He reached out and picked up a telephone. "First of all we're going to call the police," he said. "When we go to Great Yarmouth, they'll come too. And of course they'll be armed."

"They'll shoot the boy!" Lady Geranium cried.

"Spurling will fire the first shot. It'll be dark. Nobody will know what's happening. And yes! The police will open fire. With luck everyone will be killed."

"Can you be sure, sir, that the police will oblige?" the chauffeur asked.

"No, Spurling. But you'll be there. And I want you to find

the boy." Sir Hubert began to dial. "Whatever happens, you're to put a bullet between his eyes. Do you understand me?"

"Perfectly, sir." Spurling reached out and turned a switch below the television monitor.

The screen went black.

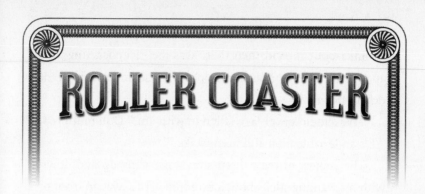

ROLLER COASTER

The first drops of rain began to fall at five to twelve. Fat and heavy, they exploded on impact like bursting tennis balls. From somewhere far away came a low, deep rumbling of thunder. It was a horrible night; hot and sticky. The sky was streaked with mauve and throbbed as if it were about to burst.

Eric and Doll Snarby were waiting in the shadows of the ghost train, the two of them jammed into a single carriage that had been decorated to resemble a vampire bat. Neither of them looked happy.

"No good will come of it," Eric was saying. "I tell you, my dear. I've got a bad feeling about this."

"Me too," Doll moaned.

"You and me . . . we was 'appier before we met Finn," Eric went on. "I mean, we was never in any trouble. A bit of shoplifting, maybe. There was always the smash-and-grabs, of course. We did thieve a couple of cars. A couple of dozen, now I think about it. And then there was the pickpocketing. But apart from that, we was honest people, you and me. Honest, decent people."

"We should never 'ave fallen in with 'im," Doll muttered. "'E's an 'orrible man and no mistake."

The subject of their discussion was pacing up and down with his walking stick about a hundred yards away in front of the roller coaster. In fact, Finn was staggering as much as pacing. He had drunk half a bottle of gin—and the other half was still in his pocket. Another great ball of rain fell down, hitting him on the shoulder. Finn swore, wiping water away from his nose and chin. Somewhere in Great Yarmouth, a clock struck midnight. Finn peered through the darkness. A car had appeared at the entrance to the boardwalk. A white Rolls-Royce.

The car stopped and Sir Hubert Spencer got out, carrying an attaché case with a silver combination lock. The thunder rumbled again.

Sir Hubert closed the door behind him and walked through the amusement park, passing between the silent machines. His feet rapped against the concrete, the sound all around him as if he were being followed by a crowd of invisible body-guards. But he seemed to be on his own. As he passed in front of the ghost train, Eric and Doll Snarby shrank from sight, then quickly looked back the way he had come. The Rolls-Royce was on its own in the street. Nothing was moving. Eric raised a hand with the thumb up. Finn saw the signal and nodded.

Neither Eric nor Finn had seen the figure who had been hiding in the back of the car. Neither of them was watching as the door slowly opened, then clicked shut again. But even as Sir Hubert Spencer walked the last few steps up to the roller coaster, Spurling slipped out of the car and hurried into the shadows. A streetlamp glimmered on something metallic that he held in his hand. But a moment later he was gone, swallowed up by the darkness.

Sir Hubert Spencer walked up to Finn and stood, towering over him. Two more different men would have been hard to imagine. Sir Hubert was dressed in an expensive raincoat, his hair immaculate, his face grim and businesslike. Finn was as sly and as shabby as ever, leaning on his walking stick, one eye blinking over the tattoo. The two of them were worlds apart, and yet as they drew close their eyes connected and each seemed to recognize something in the other.

"Good evening, Sir Hubert," Finn began.

"Let's not waste words," Sir Hubert snapped. If he had noticed Finn's peculiar tattoo, he showed no reaction. "You have my son?"

"He's safe, Sir Hubert. And very near. Do you have the particulars?"

"The what?"

"The money!"

"Where's the boy?"

"The money first!"

There was a long pause. Sir Hubert seemed unwilling to open the attaché case and suddenly Finn was suspicious. "You do have the money?" he demanded. "You haven't tried anything fancy, I take it?"

"Of course I haven't," Sir Hubert replied. "What do you think I am?"

Finn's lips stretched in a sly smile, dragging the cobweb. "Oh, I think I know what you are, Sir Hubert," he murmured. "I'd say you're pretty much the same as me, although I daresay there aren't many who'd suspect it. You're wondering how I know? Well, it takes one to know one, as my old mum used to say before she went on the bottle. Oh yes—you got your fancy title. You got a position. But I can see what's what and I can smell it too, and you're not going to try and tell me any different, are you!"

Sir Hubert laughed. "All right," he said. "Why not admit it? You're a rogue and so am I. But there is one difference between us, Mister . . ."

"Finn. Archibald Finn. What is the difference, Sir Hubert?"

"Only this." Sir Hubert's face twisted with contempt. "I am successful. Immensely, stupendously successful. But you're nothing. A petty criminal. That's the difference between us, Mr. Finn. I've gotten away with it. But you've been caught!"

Sir Hubert raised his hand and Finn shrank away, lifting his own walking stick as if in self-defense. But Sir Hubert wasn't going to hit him. The movement was only a signal. Finn saw it and understood its significance too late.

A shot rang out, astonishingly loud in the wet night air. Finn screamed as a bullet hammered into his shoulder, throwing him forward into Sir Hubert's arms. For a moment the two men stood there, locked together, their faces almost touching.

"You cheated me!" Finn whined.

"Of course I cheated you!" Sir Hubert smiled. "That's what I do!"

Desperately, Finn lunged for the attaché case and managed to rip it away from Sir Hubert's grasp. The case fell open and suddenly Finn was surrounded by hundreds of scraps of paper, tumbling and scattering around his feet. Newspaper. Sir Hubert hadn't brought a million dollars. He hadn't brought any money at all.

"No . . ." Finn whimpered. His shoulder was on fire, blood trickling down his neck.

Sir Hubert laughed a second time.

And then two searchlights exploded into life and there was the roar and clatter of engines as two police helicopters came in low, flying over the sea. Somewhere a whistle shrieked. There was another roll of thunder and immediately after it an amplified voice that could have come out of the clouds themselves.

"This is the police! Stay where you are! We are armed! Do not attempt to move!"

But Finn was already moving. Cursing and weeping at his bad luck, he had stumbled away from Sir Hubert, dropping the worthless attaché case. He had dropped his walking stick when the bullet hit him and his empty hand was clamped over the wound. Now he searched for a way out. But it was too late. Two police cars tore in from opposite directions, skidding to a halt outside the main gate. Uniformed police poured out of them while more men with dogs suddenly appeared at the edge of the park and began to spread out in a line. Then the helicopter searchlights swung in on him and Finn froze. He was trapped by the light, blinded and flattened by it like a germ on a laboratory slide.

"Stay where you are!" the voice commanded again. It was coming from the first of the helicopters that now hovered over him, whipping up the dust and sending the blank paper notes flying. "We are armed!"

For a moment Finn was lost in a dust cloud. He realized he had one chance and he took it. With a great shout he hurled himself over a low wall and onto the tracks of the roller coaster itself. And then he was away, staggering toward the corner and the first ascent. By the time the police had reached Sir Hubert, Finn had gone.

A thin gray man in a blue-and-silver uniform had marched up to Sir Hubert. This was the chief detective in charge of the operation. His name was Jones. He was in his late fifties with the drawn, skeletal face of a man who never slept. "What happened?" he demanded. "Who fired the shot?"

"It was him!" Sir Hubert replied. "He had a gun. When he saw there was no money, he tried to kill me."

"But it looked to me like he was the one who was hit, sir," Jones said.

"Yes," Sir Hubert explained. "I managed to get hold of the gun. He pulled the trigger and he hit himself."

The detective gazed at Sir Hubert. He was obviously puzzled by something. But he didn't speak.

"The man's getting away!" Sir Hubert shouted, pointing at the roller coaster. "Why don't you get after him?"

The detective nodded. Three policemen jumped over the wall and began to run down the track. All of them were armed.

Meanwhile, Finn had reached the highest point of the roller coaster, a length of track that ran flat for just a few feet before plunging down again in what would have been the biggest thrill of the ride. For a few moments he stood there, swaying. The two helicopters buzzed around him, their searchlights sweeping across him without settling on him. Finn batted at them, a miniature King Kong. They were giving him a headache. He wanted them to go away.

Climbing the track had taken all his strength. He had lost blood. There were little pools of it behind him, every few steps. He looked at it, marveling. A terrible, deafening burst of thunder came rolling in from the sea and he almost lost his balance. As he swayed on the metal track the night exploded, smashed by a massive bolt of lightning. The light danced in Finn's eyes and he sang out drunkenly.

"It's all over for you, Finn," he cried. "This time it's the end, old friend. There's nowhere for you to go now."

He glanced around, alerted by the sound of men climbing.

The three policemen were already halfway up the track, using their hands as well as their feet to move forward on the rain-swept surface.

"Go away!" he shouted. "Leave me alone!"

The policemen squatted down, their guns aimed at Finn. "Throw down your weapon!" the nearest one shouted.

Finn threw back his head and laughed. "One last drink!" he shouted, but the wind snatched away the words before they could be heard. "A toast to Sir Hubert lousy Spencer and his rotten, stinking son. And a toast to prison! Back to prison we go! Back to the old cell!"

He reached into his pocket.

The three policemen, believing he was going for his gun, opened fire as one.

For a moment Finn stood there on the track, his arms out-stretched, his face twisted in a ghastly smile as if he were wel-coming the storm and the night that was rushing in to take him. Then he plummeted forward.

Still hiding in the ghost train, Eric and Doll Snarby watched Finn as he seemed to dive into death. There was a last high-pitched scream. The two of them covered their eyes. But months later they would still be unable to sleep, remembering the dreadful thud as the body hit the ground.

The ambulance came about twenty minutes later.

With the police still combing the boardwalk, Finn was car-ried into the ambulance, his body covered by a blanket. Detec-tive Jones watched the body go. It was half past twelve but the night seemed to have gone on forever. He sighed and shook water from his head as a younger policeman approached.

"Sir?"

"Yes!"

"There's still no sign of the Snarbys, sir. But we found this . . . next to the ghost train." The policeman handed Jones a radio transmitter, dripping wet. "Apparently they've got a caravan, sir," the policeman went on. "Across the road."

Jones slid the transmitter into his pocket and nodded. "Then that's where we'll find Tad Spencer," he said.

Three minutes later, the detective and his men had the caravan surrounded. Sir Hubert Spencer had followed them over and was watching with keen, narrowed eyes. The door to the caravan was closed, but the lights were on behind the windows. Apart from the raindrops hitting the roof and bouncing off, there was no sign of movement. The rain was falling so hard now that it seemed almost solid, a single mass of water. The detective drew his raincoat around himself and shivered.

He gave a signal and about a dozen policemen hurried forward, their feet splashing down in puddles as they closed in on the caravan. But Jones wasn't taking any chances. He had guessed the kidnap victim was in the caravan but he still didn't know who might be with him. He lifted a megaphone and held it to his lips.

"This is the police!" Even amplified, his voice was almost drowned out by the rain. He turned up the volume. "The caravan's surrounded," he called out. "Open the door and come out with your hands up . . ."

The rain lashed down. The door of the caravan remained closed.

Jones sighed. He put down the megaphone and walked forward. There were just ten yards between him and the caravan. He didn't try to run.

With Sir Hubert and all the other policemen watching, he reached the door. He opened it. A dozen guns were raised. A dozen men waited to run forward.

Jones shook his head. The caravan was empty. There was nobody there.

And it was then that the radio transmitter that he had put in his pocket suddenly crackled into life. The detective pulled it out and stared at it. It was the last thing they had expected.

"This is Bob Snarby," came a voice, and it was Bob Snarby's voice even if it was Tad who really spoke. "I've got the kid and I've got a knife. I'll give 'im up . . . but only to Sir Hubert Spencer. If 'e wants the kid back, 'e'll find 'im in the Mirror Maze. Back in the park.

"We're in the Mirror Maze. But Sir Hubert's got to come alone. No tricks. I've got a knife and I'll use it. I want to see Sir Hubert and I want to see him alone."

THE MIRROR MAZE

Tad didn't have a knife.

He had guessed Sir Hubert would double-cross Finn and at ten minutes to twelve he had crept out of the caravan taking Bob Snarby—his hands still tied and his mouth gagged—with him. The two boys had been in the amusement park when Finn had fallen to his death. Afterward, they had slipped into the nearest attraction to hide.

It was only when he was inside that Tad realized where he was. Flicking on the flashlight that he had brought from the Snarbys' caravan, he had been astonished by the sight of about a thousand reflections of himself, leaping out of the darkness. He swung the flashlight left and right and was dazzled by the thousand beams of light that shone back at him. And behind the light, everywhere he looked, line after line of Tad Spencers stared back, an army of scrawny, fair-haired boys, standing there, their faces grim. And Bob Snarby was also there, of course. Line after line of him, dripping wet and shivering, his hands securely tied.

He was inside the Mirror Maze.

Tad flicked off the radio transmitter and set it down, wondering how long it would take Sir Hubert to arrive. He had no idea what would happen to him when this was all over, but he supposed he would end up in jail. He no longer cared. It seemed to him now that everything had led to this moment, a last meeting with the man who had almost had him killed. Tad knew that he couldn't go to the police. No matter how terrible his crimes, Sir Hubert was still his father. But there was one thing that he could do. Somehow he would make his father recognize him. He would tell him about the switch and everything that had happened since. He would tell him what he knew about ACID and Beautiful World.

And then he would turn his back on him and never see him again.

Outside the Mirror Maze, Sir Hubert had arrived.

He was walking with the detective, shielding himself under an umbrella as the rain crashed down. The Mirror Maze was partly surrounded by the other police officers, all of them dripping wet. As far as they were concerned, the excitement was over. Finn was dead. There was only some crazy kid to deal with. They just wanted to go home to bed.

Jones paused outside the front entrance to the Mirror Maze. "Are you sure you're going to be all right, Sir Hubert?" he asked.

Sir Hubert shook rain off his umbrella. "Don't worry, Detective." He sniffed. "I'll talk to this wretched little delinquent and see what he wants—if he even knows himself. I'll talk him out into the open and then you and your men can deal with him."

"He did say he had a knife, sir," Jones reminded him. "And there's still the matter of the gun."

"What gun?" Sir Hubert asked.

Jones looked at Sir Hubert curiously, as if he were trying to look through him. "The gun that you said Finn had, sir. Somebody fired a shot, but we still haven't found the gun . . ."

Sir Hubert smiled. "I'm not afraid," he said. "If the boy's got a gun, so much the worse for him." He stepped forward eagerly. "Now let's get this over with. I've wasted enough time with this young street urchin already."

As Sir Hubert approached the entrance, another figure flitted out of the shelter of the bumper cars and ran the few paces to the back of the Mirror Maze. Nobody saw him. The man worked quickly, using a screwdriver to pry three wooden planks away from the rear wall. This made a hole large enough to slip through even though this was an unusually large man.

Spurling. Sir Hubert's chauffeur.

He tore his uniform as he squeezed inside and for a moment his arm hung outside in the rain with his sleeve caught on a nail. Water dripped off his hand and the cold metal barrel of the gun it was holding. Then he unhooked himself. He pulled the gun in. And turned to find the boy he had come to kill.

. . .

Sir Hubert let the door swing shut behind him and stood in utter darkness. He listened for any sound of movement, but the rain beating down on the roof and walls would have muffled it anyway.

"Is there anybody there?" he called out. "Bob Snarby? I understand that's your name. Do you want to speak to me?"

Silence. The darkness unnerved him. But just before the door had closed, he had noticed a bank of electric switches set to one side and now he groped for them. He flicked one of them on, but there was still no light. Sir Hubert thought he heard something—a faint electronic whine—but against the pattering of the rain it was hard to be sure. He left the switch down and found another. This time a single red bulb came on, high above the mirrors.

It was enough. Sir Hubert found himself facing a corridor of glass that broke off immediately in three different directions. There were panels everywhere. Some were transparent, some were mirrors. If you moved forward too quickly you could easily crash into an invisible barrier—or into a reflection of yourself. The light that Sir Hubert had turned on wasn't strong enough to reach the outer walls of the Mirror Maze. The deep red glow spread out in a wide circle. But the mirrors, the sweeping corridors, seemed to go on forever.

And everywhere he looked, Sir Hubert saw the faces of the three people who had finally come together.

One thousand Tad Spencers.

One thousand Bob Snarbys.

One thousand Sir Huberts.

Reflections of reflections of reflections.

"Bob Snarby," Sir Hubert said.

"I'm not Bob Snarby. I'm Tad. I'm your son."

Sir Hubert didn't understand. It was the rough-looking boy who had spoken, the one with the studs in his ear. His son couldn't speak. He was gagged.

"You tried to kill me," Tad said.

Sir Hubert said nothing. He would let the boy talk. A few more seconds and Spurling would be ready.

"When I was in the Center . . . I couldn't believe it was you. I didn't want to believe it! My own dad. Doing experiments on kids off the street. It was like I was seeing you for the first time—and what I saw . . . it was horrible!"

"I'm not your father!" Sir Hubert snapped. He took a step forward and cried out loud as he banged into a sheet of glass. He spun around. The reflections watched him.

"I know about the Indians too," Tad went on. "The Arambayans." Dragging Bob with him, he made his way to the very center of the maze. He felt safer here, with glass all around. "How could you do that, Dad?" he shouted. "Kill all those people just to make money! Didn't you have enough?"

"There's no such thing as enough!" Sir Hubert shouted back. "And why do you call me your father?"

"Because you are!"

"No. You have my son with you. This whole thing is ri-

151

diculous. Let him go and we can straighten this all out. Nobody's going to hurt you." He took another step forward. All around, his reflections moved as well.

"Stay where you are!" Tad also moved and once again the patterns shifted, endless lines of men and lines of boys crossing and recrossing one another in the Mirror Maze. "Admit it!" he cried. "I admired you so much, but it was all a lie. You're a criminal. Worse than Finn!"

And then Sir Hubert saw it. A fourth image had appeared in the mirrors, on the very edge of the red circle . . . a huddled shape reflected around and around. Had the boy seen him? Of course he had. But there was nothing he could do. Sir Hubert allowed himself a thin, cruel smile. Spurling was here. It was finally over.

"You want me to tell you the truth?" Sir Hubert called out. "It's my pleasure!" He slammed his hand against a mirror. A thousand hands thundered at a thousand reflections of Tad. "Yes—boy—you have learned rather too much about me. My little experiments in the Center? How else can I be sure that my products are safe? The stupid public gets all upset when it's rabbits or mice or monkeys on the operating table, but who cares about delinquent children dragged off the London streets? Homeless, hopeless children like you? So—yes—my charity, ACID, turned you into a laboratory rat as it has done a hundred children before you. It's all you deserve."

"And you kill people!" Tad cried, horrified and sickened by what he was hearing. "The Arambayans—"

"Primitives! Savages! Animals!" Sir Hubert laughed. "They

wouldn't sell me what I wanted, so of course I had them wiped out. Do you think anybody cares? When people pay seventeen dollars and fifty cents for a bottle of Moonfruit Massage, they're not thinking of a tribe of Indians on the other side of the world! Nobody ever thinks of anybody else. That's what capitalism is all about!"

Once more the pattern changed. A thousand guns took aim.

"Kill him, Spurling!" Sir Hubert snapped. "He knows about me. I want him dead!"

"Kill him, Spurling! I want him dead!"

The words echoed all around the fairgrounds just as every word had echoed ever since Sir Hubert had accidentally turned on the loudspeakers in the Mirror Maze. The police had heard everything. Sir Hubert Spencer had confessed to unspeakable crimes. Experimenting on children! Genocide! And now attempted murder.

The detective was the first to react. While everyone else just stood there, as if in shock, he ran forward, heading for the entrance to the maze.

Inside, Spurling's finger tightened on the trigger. A single bead of sweat drew a careful line down his forehead. His target was only a few yards away from him. But which target? Where should he fire?

"Kill him!" Sir Hubert shouted again.

Tad was utterly surrounded by guns. They were in front of him, behind him, above him and below him. He spun around, trying to find a way out, but now he realized that he too was trapped in the Mirror Maze. His fists struck out at the glass walls. They seemed to have closed in on him, boxing him in.

"Mmmm . . ." Bob Snarby shook his head from side to side and at last he managed to get his shoulder to the gag, dragging it off. The guns seemed to be pointing at him too and his eyes bulged with fear.

The detective kicked open the door of the Mirror Maze and ran in. He shouted two words. "Sir Hubert!"

Spurling fired.

And everywhere mirrors smashed as, one after another, the bullet tunneled through them, each tiny hole becoming a thousand tiny holes in the reflections as spidery cracks—millions of them—splintered out in all directions. At the same time there was one last great burst of thunder that smashed through the clouds and shook the entire building.

Tad cried out as the bullet hit him, throwing him off his feet. The pain was like nothing he had ever experienced. He felt every tiny millimeter of the bullet's progress as it passed through his skin, his flesh, his muscle and his bone. His shoulders hit the mirror behind him and he slid down, trailing blood behind him. The thunder pounded at his ears and there was a flash of lightning worse than any that had come before, slicing into his eyes, blinding him.

At the same instant Bob Snarby screamed too.

Tad reached the ground, one leg bent under him, the other outstretched. And in the last few seconds before darkness came, he saw what had happened.

A uniformed policeman. Spurling with the gun. Sir Hubert, his eyes staring, photographed a thousand times.

Then a gunshot. Two more. Two thousand sparks of flame. Mirrors shattering. Spurling's reflection falling back and disappearing.

Suddenly there was no more pain. Tad closed his eyes. Suddenly there wasn't anything.

The boy with fair hair and two studs in his ear shivered and lay still.

TOGETHER

The St. Elizabeth Institute for Juvenile Care was
a plain, modern building in Sourbridge, on the outskirts of
Birmingham. It didn't quite look like a prison—there were no
bars on the windows—but it was just about as welcoming. The
front was bare brick, the doors solid steel. The institute had
been built on the edge of a busy road, but as the traffic thundered past, nobody turned to look at it. It was the sort of place
that had been designed not to be seen.

Three months after the shoot-out on Great Yarmouth
boardwalk, with the last of the summer hanging in the air, a
boy stepped out of a door at the back of the institute and stood
in front of the fenced-in square of asphalt that was the soccer
field, the exercise yard and the garden for those who lived inside. The boy was fourteen years old with short black hair.
Although he was dressed in the pale blue shirt and denim

pants that was the uniform of the St. Elizabeth Institute, there was something about him that suggested he was used to more comfortable clothes.

The boy's name was Thomas Arnold David Spencer. He paused outside the door as if looking for someone. Then he started to walk forward.

There was a second boy sitting on a bench at the far end of the yard, also dressed in a blue shirt and denim pants, his arm in a sling, chewing gum. This boy was much thinner than the other and had long, fair hair.

Hearing the footsteps approach, Bob Snarby turned around. He seemed to take a long time to recognize Tad, and when he did finally speak, his voice was unfriendly. "What are you doing here?"

"I've been sent here," Tad said.

"What? You're living here too?"

"Yes. I just got here today."

"So what happened to your mum and dad? Sir Hubert and Lady Moneybags. And what about Snatchmore Hall?"

"Snatchmore Hall's up for sale," Tad replied. "My parents are in jail."

And it was true. Tad Spencer was back in his own body. Bob Snarby was back in his. But everything in the lives of both boys had changed.

Tad still didn't know how he had switched places again—whether it was the storm or the shock of the bullet that had hit him. He even wondered if Dr. Aftexcludor hadn't played a part in it. After all, with Sir Hubert's confession and subsequent arrest, the Arambayans had been avenged and hadn't that been the whole point?

He hadn't died in the Mirror Maze. What he had experienced was the jolting, terrible power of the switch as it fell on him a second time, sucking him out of Bob's body and sending him back to his own. He had thought he was dying. But seconds later he had stood up, his arms tied behind him. He was unhurt.

It was Bob Snarby who had been rushed to a hospital and emergency surgery and for the next week had remained in a critical condition. But Bob had always been tough. Slowly he had begun to recover and four weeks later the doctors were finished with him. He was allowed out of the hospital. Eric and Doll Snarby weren't there to greet him.

For the Snarbys had both disappeared. Although the police had discovered several cigarette butts and a cold steak-and-kidney pie in the ghost train, Eric and Doll had simply vanished into thin air. There had since been a few sightings of them in Ireland, a huge, fat woman and a balding little man, working as fish-and-chip sellers in a food truck. Apparently there were never any chips, as the woman constantly ate them all. But since then they had moved on again. The police had given up hope of arresting them.

Spurling was dead. He had made the mistake of turning his gun on the police and the detective—who was also armed—had shot him in self-defense. The chauffeur had been buried a few days later in the same cemetery as Finn.

With the arrest of Sir Hubert and Lady Geranium Spencer, Beautiful World had collapsed. NONE OF OUR PRODUCTS ARE TESTED ON ANIMALS. When the truth about the tests had become known, the entire country had recoiled in horror. Several of the stores were actually burned down by furious, shouting crowds. The police had raided the Center, freeing the children who were still there and making over a dozen arrests. Sir Hubert's knighthood had of course been withdrawn. He was now just plain Hubert Spencer: prisoner 7430909 in Wormwood Scrubs—where he was sentenced to remain for the next ninety years.

It had been one final twist of fate that had thrown the two boys together.

The police had decided to overlook Bob's part in the kidnapping and the break-in at the house of Lord Roven. He had, after all, been under Finn's influence and Finn had now paid for his crimes. It was quickly decided that Bob should be put into a group home. But Tad too had no parents and nowhere to go. His was a more difficult case in that he did have relatives who could look after him, but unfortunately they had all disowned him, not wanting to be involved in the scandal. His file had been passed around from committee to committee, but eventually he had been put into a home as well.

Both boys had been sent to the St. Elizabeth Institute. They had arrived on the same day.

Now Tad waited for Bob to speak. Bob gazed at the other boy. His face was blank, neither hostile nor friendly. "You aren't so fat anymore," he said.

Tad shrugged. "I've been doing more exercise. And I don't eat so much now."

"And you've 'ad your ear done."

"Yes." There was a silver stud in Tad's right ear. He rubbed it gently. "I got to like having one." He paused. "There were quite a lot of things I liked about being you, Bob."

"Well, you're not me anymore," the other boy snapped. "So why 'ave you come looking for me? Come to 'ave a good laugh?"

"I've got nothing to laugh about," Tad replied. "I'm the same as you now. My parents are gone and it looks like I'm stuck here." He sighed. "Bob, I came to say I'm sorry."

"Sorry?"

"It was me who Spurling came to kill. And it was me who should have got shot. I suppose I did. But it was you who had all the pain, the hospital, all the rest of it. I didn't know we were going to switch back again . . ."

"It certainly couldn't 'ave happened at a worse time," Bob agreed. He swung around—but slowly. "So you're stuck here, are you?"

Tad nodded. "I don't care," he said. "I couldn't have gone back home anyway, even if Snatchmore Hall hadn't been put up for sale."

"Didn't you 'ave uncles? Aunts?"

"They didn't want me." Tad looked around him and sighed. "I might as well stay here as anywhere," he said. "It's only for two years. Then I'll be sixteen and they'll have to let me out. And then I can start again."

Tad fell silent. There were a few trees near the yard, their leaves turning gold with the arrival of autumn. Behind them he could see the sun, already beginning to set.

"So what now?" Bob Snarby asked.

"I hoped we could be friends," Tad said.

"What? You 'n me?"

"Why not?" Tad sat down next to Bob. "Nobody's ever known each other as well as you and I have. I mean, we've actually *been* each other."

"Did you ever tell anyone?" Bob Snarby asked.

"About the switch?" Tad shook his head. "No. I didn't think anyone would believe me."

"Me neither."

"It's only two years," Tad went on. "And then we'll be on our own. No parents. No Finn. Nobody to tell us what to do or turn us into what they want us to be. In some ways, maybe that's the best thing that ever happened to me."

"Yeah? And what then?" Bob wasn't convinced. "What do you think will happen to us then? You say you're the same as me now. Well, what chance do you think people like us ever have?"

"I think we can be anything we want to be," Tad replied. "If we stick together. And if we want it hard enough. With what you know and what I know . . . together we can take on the world."

Bob smiled for the first time. "Listen to you!" he said. "I bet you was never like this before you was me."

"I bet you've changed too."

"Yeah. Maybe." Bob shrugged ruefully—the movement made him wince. "You know, in the end I didn't much like being you," he admitted. "It was lovely to start with. Like having Christmas every day. But can you imagine Christmas every day? How bored you'd get? I was beginning to feel like I was drowning. No wonder you were the way you were. You were spoiled rotten."

"Eric and Doll weren't great parents either."

"That's true."

Bob stood up. Tad helped him get to his feet, then held out a hand. "Friends?" he asked.

Bob Snarby took the hand. They shook.

A bell rang inside the institute and together they began to walk back.

They had been each other and now they were themselves. But best of all they were together, and as they slowly crossed the exercise yard, walking side by side, Tad was filled with hope and with happiness, knowing in his heart that the adventure of his life had only now begun.

Turn the page for a preview of

STORMBREAKER

1
FUNERAL VOICES

WHEN THE DOORBELL rings at three in the morning, it's never good news.

Alex Rider was woken by the first chime. His eyes flickered open, but for a moment he stayed completely still in his bed, lying on his back with his head resting on the pillow. He heard a bedroom door open and a creak of wood as somebody went downstairs. The bell rang a second time, and he looked at the alarm clock glowing beside him. There was a rattle as someone slid the security chain off the front door.

He rolled out of bed and walked over to the open window, his bare feet pressing down the carpet pile. The moonlight spilled onto his chest and shoulders. Alex was fourteen, already well built, with the body of an athlete. His hair, cut short apart from two thick strands hanging over his forehead, was fair. His eyes were brown and serious. For a moment he stood silently, half hidden in the shadow, looking out. There was a police car parked outside. From his second-floor window Alex could see the black ID number on the roof and the caps of the two men who were standing in front of the door. The porch light went on and, at the same time, the door opened.

"Mrs. Rider?"

"No. I'm the housekeeper. What is it? What's happened?"

"This is the home of Mr. Ian Rider?"

"Yes."

"I wonder if we could come in . . ."

And Alex already knew. He knew from the way the police stood there, awkward and unhappy. But he also knew from the tone of their voices. Funeral voices . . . that was how he would describe them later. The sort of voices people use when they come to tell you that someone close to you has died.

He went to his door and opened it. He could hear the two policemen talking down in the hall, but only some of the words reached him.

". . . a car accident . . . called the ambulance . . . intensive care . . . nothing anyone could do . . . so sorry."

It was only hours later, sitting in the kitchen, watching as the gray light of morning bled slowly through the West London streets, that Alex could try to make sense of what had happened. His uncle—Ian Rider—was dead. Driving home, his car had been hit by a truck at Old Street roundabout and he had been killed almost instantly. He hadn't been wearing a seat belt, the police said. Otherwise, he might have had a chance.

Alex thought of the man who had been his only relation for as long as he could remember. He had never known his own parents. They had both died in another accident, this one a plane crash, a few weeks after he had been born. He had been brought up by his father's brother (never "uncle"—Ian Rider had hated that word) and had spent fourteen years in the same terraced house in Chelsea, London, between the King's Road and the river. The two of them had always been close. Alex remembered the vacations they'd taken together, the many sports they'd played, the movies they'd seen. They hadn't just been relations, they'd been friends. It was almost impossible to imagine that he would never again see the man, hear his laughter, or twist his arm to get help with his science homework.

Alex sighed, fighting against the sense of grief that was suddenly overwhelming. But what saddened him the most was the realization—too late now—that despite everything, he had hardly known his uncle at all.

He was a banker. People said Alex looked a little like him. Ian Rider was always traveling. A quiet, private man who liked good wine, classical music, and books. Who didn't seem to have any girlfriends . . . in fact, he didn't have any friends at all. He had kept himself fit, had never smoked, and had dressed expensively. But that wasn't enough. It wasn't a picture of a life. It was only a thumbnail sketch.

"Are you all right, Alex?" A young woman had come into the room. She was in her late twenties with a sprawl of red hair and a round, boyish face. Jack Starbright was American. She had come to London as a student seven years ago, rented a room in the house—in return for light housework and baby-sitting duties—and had stayed on to become housekeeper and one of Alex's closest companions. Sometimes he wondered what the Jack was short for. Jackie? Jacqueline? Neither of them suited her and although he had once asked, she had never said.

Alex nodded. "What do you think will happen?" he asked.

"What do you mean?"

"To the house. To me. To you."

"I don't know." She shrugged. "I guess Ian would have made a will," she said. "He'll have left instructions."

"Maybe we should look in his office."

"Yeah. But not today, Alex. Let's take it one step at a time."

Ian's office was a room running the full length of the house, high up on the top. It was the only room that was always locked—Alex had only been in there three or four times, and never on his own. When he was younger, he had fantasized that there might be something strange up there . . . a time machine or a UFO. But it was merely an office with a desk, a couple of filing cabinets, shelves full of papers and books. Bank stuff—that's what Ian said. Even so, Alex wanted to go up there now.

"The police said he wasn't wearing his seat belt." Alex turned to look at Jack.

She nodded. "Yeah. That's what they said."

"Doesn't that seem strange to you? You know how careful he was. He always wore his seat belt. He wouldn't even drive me around the corner without making me put mine on."

Jack thought for a moment, then shrugged. "Yeah, it is strange," she said. "But that must have been the way it was. Why would the police have lied?"

The day dragged on. Alex hadn't gone to school even though, secretly, he wanted to. He would have preferred to escape back into normal life, the clang of the bell, the crowds of familiar faces, instead of sitting here, trapped inside the house. But he had to be there for the visitors who came throughout the morning and the rest of the afternoon.

There were five of them. A lawyer who knew nothing about any will but seemed to have been charged with organizing the funeral. A funeral director who had been recommended by the lawyer. A vicar—tall, elderly—who seemed disappointed that Alex refused to cry. A neighbor from across the road—how did she even know that anyone had died? And finally a man from the bank.

"All of us at the Royal and General are deeply shocked," he said. He looked about thirty, wearing a polyester suit with a Marks & Spencer tie. He had the sort of face you forget even while you're looking at it and had introduced himself as Crawley, from personnel. "But if there's anything we can do . . ."

"What will happen?" Alex asked for the second time that day.

"You don't have to worry," Crawley said. "The bank will take care of everything. That's my job. You leave everything to me."

The day passed. Alex killed a couple of hours knocking a few balls around on his uncle's snooker table—and then felt vaguely guilty when Jack caught him at it. But what else was he to do? Later on she took him to a Burger King. He was glad to get out of the house, but the two of them barely spoke. Alex assumed Jack would have to go back to America. She certainly couldn't stay in London forever. So who would look after him? At fourteen, he was still too young to look after himself. His whole future looked so uncertain that he preferred not to talk about it. He preferred not to talk at all.

And then the day of the funeral arrived and Alex found himself dressed in a dark jacket and cords, preparing to leave in a black car that had come from nowhere surrounded by people he had never met. Ian Rider was buried in Brompton Cemetery on the Fulham Road, just in the shadow of the Chelsea soccer field, and Alex knew where he would have preferred to be on that warm Wednesday afternoon. About thirty people had turned up, but he hardly recognized any of them. A grave had been dug close to the lane that ran the length of the cemetery, and as the service began, a black Rolls-Royce drew up, the back door opened, and a man got out. Alex watched him as he walked forward and stopped. Alex shivered. There was something about the new arrival that made his skin crawl.

And yet the man was ordinary to look at. Gray suit, gray hair, gray lips, and gray eyes. His face was expressionless, the eyes behind the square, gunmetal spectacles, completely empty. Perhaps that was what had disturbed Alex. Whoever this man was, he seemed to have less life than anyone in the cemetery. Above or below ground.

Someone tapped Alex on the shoulder and he turned around to see Mr. Crawley leaning over him. "That's Mr. Blunt," the personnel manager whispered. "He's the chairman of the bank."

Alex's eyes traveled past Blunt and over to the Rolls-Royce. Two more men had come with him, one of them driving. They were wearing identical suits and, although it wasn't a particularly bright day, sun-glasses. Both of them were watching the funeral with the same grim faces. Alex looked from them to Blunt and then to the other people who had come to the cemetery. Had they really known Ian Rider? Why had he never met any of them before? And why did he find it so difficult to believe that they really worked for a bank?

". . . a good man, a patriotic man. He will be missed."

The vicar had finished his graveside address. His choice of words struck Alex as odd. Patriotic? That meant he loved his country. But as far as Alex knew, Ian Rider had barely spent any time in it. Certainly he had never been one for waving the Union Jack. He looked around, hoping to find Jack, but saw instead that Blunt was making his way toward him, stepping carefully around the grave.

"You must be Alex." The chairman was only a little taller than him. Up close, his skin was strangely unreal. It could have been made of plastic. "My name is Alan Blunt," he said. "Your uncle often spoke about you."

"That's funny," Alex said. "He never mentioned you."

The gray lips twitched briefly. "We'll miss him. He was a good man."

"What was he good at?" Alex asked. "He never talked about his work."

Suddenly Crawley was there. "Your uncle was overseas finance manager, Alex," he said. "He was responsible for our foreign branches. You must have known that."

"I know he traveled a lot," Alex said. "And I know he was very careful. About things like seat belts."

"Well, sadly, he wasn't careful enough." Blunt's eyes, magnified by the thick lenses of his spectacles, lasered into his own, and for a moment, Alex felt himself pinned down, like an insect under a microscope. "I hope we'll meet again," Blunt went on. He tapped the side of his face with a single gray finger. "Yes . . ." Then he turned and went back to his car.

That was when it happened. As Blunt was getting into the Rolls-Royce, the driver leaned down to open the back door and his jacket fell open, revealing a stark white shirt underneath. There was a black shape lying against it and that was what caught Alex's eye. The man was wearing a leather holster with an automatic pistol strapped inside. Realizing what had hap-

pened, the driver quickly straightened up and pulled
the jacket across. Blunt had seen it too. He turned
back and looked again at Alex. Something very close
to an emotion slithered over his face. Then he got
into the car, the door closed, and he was gone.

A gun at a funeral, Alex thought. Why? Why
should bank managers carry guns?

"Let's get out of here." Suddenly Jack was at his
side. "Cemeteries give me the creeps."

"Yes. And quite a few creeps have turned up,"
Alex muttered.

They slipped away quietly and went home. The
car that had taken them to the funeral was still waiting, but they preferred the open air. The walk took
them fifteen minutes and as they turned the corner
onto their street, Alex noticed a moving van parked in
front of the house, the words STRYKER & SON painted
on its side.

"What's that doing . . .?" he began.

At the same moment, the van shot off, the wheels
skidding over the surface of the road.

Alex said nothing as Jack unlocked the door and
let them in, but while she went into the kitchen to
make some tea, he quickly looked around the house.

A letter that had been on the hall table now lay on the carpet. A door that had been half open was now closed. Tiny details, but Alex's eyes missed nothing. Somebody had been in the house. He was almost sure of it.

But he wasn't certain until he got to the top floor. The door to the office, which had always, always been locked, was now unlocked. Alex opened it and went in. The room was empty. Ian Rider had gone and so had everything else. The desk drawers, the closets, the shelves . . . anything connected to the dead man's work had been taken. Whatever the truth was about his uncle's past, someone had just wiped it out.

POINT BLANK

When an investigation into a series of mysterious deaths turns up one common link, fourteen-year-old DDIaddiereluctant spy Alex Rider is tapped to investigate. Trapped in a remote boarding school high atop the Swiss Alps among the sons of the richest and most powerful families, Alex knows something is wrong. Very wrong. These former juvenile delinquents have turned well-behaved, studious—and identical—overnight. And it's up to Alex to find out who is behind this nefarious plot, before they find him. The clock is ticking, and Alex's luck is about to run out.

PB: 978-0-14-240612-0

SKELETON KEY

Working as a secret agent for Britain's most exclusive agency, Alex Rider has seen it all. He's been shot at by international terrorists, stood face-to-face with pure evil, and saved the world—twice. All before his fifteenth birthday. But Alex is about to face something more dangerous than he can imagine: a man who's lost everything he cared for—his country, his son—a man who has a nuclear weapon, and will stop at nothing to get his world back. Unless Alex can stop him first. . . .

PB: 978-0-14-240614-7

EAGLE STRIKE

Sir Damian Cray is a philanthropist, a peace activist, and the world's most famous pop star. But still it's not enough. He needs more if he is to save the world. Trouble is, only Alex Rider recognizes that it's the world that needs saving from Sir Damian Cray. Underneath the luster of glamour and fame lies a twisted mind, ready to sacrifice the world for his beliefs. But in the past, Alex has always had the backing of the government. This time, he's on his own. Can one teenager convince the world that the most popular man on earth is a madman bent on destruction—before time runs out?

PB: 978-0-14-240613-9

SCORPIA

Alex Rider, teen spy, has always been told he is the spitting image of the father he never knew. But then Alex learns that his father may have been an assassin for the most lethal and powerful terrorist organization in the world, Scorpia. Now Scorpia wants Alex on their side, and Alex no longer has the strength to fight them. That is, until he learns of Scorpia's latest plot: an operation known only as "Invisible Sword" that will result in the death of thousands of people. Can Alex prevent the slaughter, or will Scorpia prove once and for all that the terror will not be stopped?

PB: 978-0-14-240578-9

ARK ANGEL

When kidnappers attempt to snatch the son of Niko-lai Drevin, one of the richest men in the world, Alex Rider knows he has to stop them. The eccentric bil-lionaire has been targeted by Force Three, a group of eco-terrorists who claim his project Ark Angel—the first luxury hotel in outer space—is a danger to the environment. Soon Alex discovers that Force Three will stop at nothing to destroy Ark Angel . . . unless Alex can stop them.

PB: 978-0-14-240738-7

SNAKEHEAD

When Alex Rider crash-lands off the coast of Australia, the Australian Secret Service recruits him to infiltrate one of the ruthless gangs operating across Southeast Asia. Known as snakeheads, the gangs smuggle drugs, weapons, and, worst of all, people. Alex accepts the assignment, in part for the chance to work with his godfather and learn more about his parents. What he uncovers, however, is a secret that will make this his darkest and most dangerous mission yet. . . .

PB: 978-0-14-241212-1